## *What Reviewers are saying For…*

"Ms. Midway has written ... that is impossible to put down. Fiona and Ned's relationship builds to an exciting climax that will have you reading until the final word."

*5 Coffee Cups, Sherry*
*Coffee Time Romance*

"An eroticized version of the office, That's What Friend's Are For, is a shining star and one of the best contemporaries to grace the pile of TBRs (To Be Reads) on my laptop this year."

*5 Unicorns, Rachelle*
*Enchanted in Romance*

"I always have a soft spot for those who can make me laugh with amazing regularity and Bridget Midway is one of those such people. Not only is her depiction of passion and love so remarkable but she pours her heart and soul into each of these novels."

*Carrie White*
*One Reviewer*

"I thought this book rocked! I was hooked from the get go. That's What Friends Are For has sweet romance, hot sex, humor, and friendship. The story just flowed and was a pleasure to read. Wonderful book!"

*5 Stars-Excellent, Christy*
*May Reviews*

Standing in the doorway, Fiona folded her arms, leaned against the frame and said, "It all makes sense. I'll show up with you at company functions so people can see me. You'll look like the company stud and it'll guarantee you more interest from your bosses. They'll notice your work, and you'll get that raise and a promotion."

If she knew what the prospect was doing to Ned, she would have known he'd been getting a raise from her since she pressed her body against him in the kitchen. ...

"And what will having sex do for my career? My ego, I know. But my career..."

"That's a no-brainer. Having sex is exactly like work. Positions. Knowing what works for your partner. Intensity. Relief."

Ned held up his hand, uncovering his growing erection. "That's enough."

Fiona pulled out a couple of twenties from his wallet for dinner and tossed the black leather billfold on his bed next to him.

"I get where you're going with this. But what will this deal do for you?"

"A nice little letter from your boss. If I can get the man alone, I can convince him to write a recommendation for me to send to Judge Kristoff. Your boss may be a slime bucket, but I bet he's got Kristoff's ear. Don't you see? This could work."

"But what about our agreement? We've remained great friends because we promised never to date and ruin our relationship."

"But this isn't sex for pleasure."

"At least with me it wouldn't be." Ned chuckled, making Fiona smile.

"This is work," she went on. "Like preparing for a job interview."

# That's What Friends Are For

By

Bridget Midway

Liquid Silver Books
Indianapolis, Indiana

Published By:
Liquid Silver Books
10509 Sedgegrass Dr.
Indianapolis, IN 46235

Liquid Silver Books publishes books online and in trade paperback. Visit our site at http://www.liquidsilverbooks.com

Manufactured in the United States of America

ISBN: 1-59578-235-4

Cover: April Martinez

# That's What Friends Are For

## *Dedication*

This book is for anyone who believes that they are defined by what other people think. Live free and be proud! I thank my mother, Ireleen, for instilling those values in me. And I thank Jimmy who has always believed in me ... and still loves me even though I'm a big nerd!

# Chapter 1

## Making a business plan

Ned Cholurski would have rather stayed at home, thinking about his sexy roommate and jerking off than be at work. But then again, he would have rather put a blowtorch to his eyes than be at work. Thinking of his roommate proved to be a better distraction.

No matter what he was doing, thoughts of Fiona flooded his mind. The way her short, sassy hair danced on her head whenever she moved made him want to run his fingers through it, get lost in the soft curls and waves like a surfer without his board. Her round, firm ass bounced through his head. And her tits. Those luscious full breasts with their dark, hard nipples made him drool.

Just envisioning her now made his cock twitch to attention. Coughing, he pressed his hand on his growing erection.

Come on, man. Keep it together. You can't pop a woody at work.

Lately, she'd skipped through his thoughts a lot. Well, was fifty times a minute a lot? It didn't help that she'd been his absolute best friend in the world since high school.

Instead of dwelling on his dilemma, he applauded at the end of his boss' lengthy, dry, redundant speech, though what he really wanted to do involved shoving a pointed stick into his eyes and ears. Could anyone keep himself sustained with that much hot air bubbling inside like his boss?

Ned watched the bloated man, Frank Chunti, or Fat Bastard as Ned liked to think of him, rear back on his heels at the end of the long conference table. The shiny mahogany warped Chunti's reflection, making him appear even more distorted and twisted. Perhaps the true man existed in the image and the fake one stood before them. His boss' face squished into a tight fist, almost obliterating his eyes. Fat Bastard.

"Great speech," one of Ned's coworkers muttered, standing. "Just a lot of doubletalk on how we're not getting raises again this year."

"Yeah," Ned piped in as he got up behind him.

The claps echoed off of the peach-colored walls decorated with amateurish paintings of what an artist must have thought the Virginia Beach coastline looked like. The painter had obviously never visited the beach during tourist season.

"Meanwhile Chunti is on his third Alfa Romeo this year. Prick," a female coworker added.

Ned never bothered learning any of his coworkers' names. Why should he? He'd hoped one day he would have been gone from this particular circle of hell, also known as Meta Corporation. He knew if he didn't leave soon he would be buried under his gray cubicle, his nameplate his tombstone.

"Third one, huh?" Ned said, trying hard to fit in but as usual, failing miserably.

The woman glared at Ned, snorted and returned her attention to their boss. In turn, because Ned never bothered learning anyone's names or joined the office lottery pool or even pitched in to the birthday fund, no one paid much attention to him.

At one time he thought he'd overheard the other employees calling him 'the tall, skinny one.' That's okay. At least they didn't call him 'potential sniper guy.'

Besides, he'd renamed them all, too. Like the woman who'd just given him a dismissive look, she was Too Much Perfume. The guy who'd commented about the raises, Nose-Picker. Instead of Native Americans they were Native Office Cubists.

He observed them like a zoologist watching a panda. Studying them had helped Ned pass the time when he'd stopped counting the ceiling tiles while a program loaded.

Too Much Perfume's small breasts sagged so much it didn't look like she ever wore a bra. Or maybe her job included smuggling chicken cutlets. And Dandruff Woman had an impossibly flat ass. Office Thief smuggled enough copier paper, pens and staples to start her own store.

Why couldn't all women look like his best friend? It was a high standard. He understood that. Maybe if he hadn't compared every woman to her, he would have dated more often.

Hell, who was he kidding? If a woman wasn't a carbon copy of his roommate, he didn't give her a second glance. He needed to, though. No way in the world would he and his best friend ever date. They'd promised each other they wouldn't ruin their friendship by turning it into something romantic.

At least that was what she'd told him. But Ned knew better. She'd known him since high school. He'd been the school nerd. Ned the Nerd. He still cringed when he thought of that nickname. And she'd been the head cheerleader and prom queen, no less. It still amazed him that they became friends at all.

The crowd dispersed, returning to their desks, including Ned, and not a moment too soon. The stench of laziness and lack of motivation, something that resembled the aroma of bleach and old papers, choked him until he got into a coughing jag that lasted all the way back to his desk. He took a sip of his water, cracked his knuckles and prepared to work.

Right after he sat in his rolling chair, he wheeled himself closer to his computer. A hand clamped on his shoulder. Turning, he caught the squinty gaze of Fat Bastard.

"Nick, good to see you again," Bastard said and gave Ned two Vulcan pinch-type squeezes to his shoulder.

"It's Ned," he said as he attempted to stand.

Bastard pressed his hand down harder, securing Ned to his spot. Ned had been told that Chunti didn't like tall people so he wouldn't have to keep looking up. It wasn't Ned's fault that at six-foot-three he was nearly a foot taller than his boss.

Glossing over the error with Ned's name, Bastard continued. "So what did you think of my little speech?"

I think I'm a better orator than you. I think no one here respects you. I think pure shit rolls from your mouth and no amount of mouthwash or toothpaste can get rid of that smell. And I think I can run this department, this company, better than you!

"It elicited a lot of strong reactions from your employees." Ned watched Bastard's face twist in a confused expression until a strained smile hitched its way up.

"Keep up the good work, Nate." And with a condescending smack to the back of Ned's neck, Bastard rolled on to the next unsuspecting victim.

Although gray surrounded him--his desk, the walls of his cubicle, even his chair--Ned saw red. He took in a deep breath, held it until the count of ten then released it through his nose in one smooth exhalation.

God, he needed a boost. He couldn't wait to get home. At least he would have something pleasant to look at, or at least someone.

* ~ *

Fiona Griffen clicked her ballpoint pen in rapid succession as she sat with the phone receiver to her ear, the drone of Muzak making her take a hold of a short curl in her hair and twirl it within an inch of its existence. Crossing her leg, she bounced it then chewed her bottom lip.

Come on. Just give me the bad news already.

Wasn't it enough that she'd gotten good grades? Good? Hell, they were great. And she'd had the bomb internships, all at active, busy courtrooms. All she wanted was this one clerk position.

Well, that wasn't all she wanted. But for her career path, it was enough for now.

What she really wanted involved perfection: the perfect job; the perfect house; the perfect car; the perfect, finest man, a man who was courteous, kind, funny, compassionate, and having a big dick wouldn't hurt either. Just as she suppressed a chuckle the Muzak thankfully stopped.

"Miss Griffen?" a voice said, breaking her frantic thoughts.

Fiona sat up straighter, took a deep breath and kept the exhalation from the mouthpiece. "Yes."

"We'll get back to you." The woman hung up.

Fiona stared at the receiver as though it would transform into a snake and strike her eyes. The tension suddenly broke; starting from her toes and coursing all the way through her body, she released a blood-curdling scream. So loud was her yell, she didn't catch the door opening and closing.

"Whoa!"

Fiona slammed the phone on the couch then turned to her roommate. "Hey, Neddy."

No matter what turmoil swirled in her life, her roommate and best friend since high school, Ned Cholurski, could always lift her spirits. This time, though, she wasn't sure if his sweet face could cheer her.

"Beer. Gin. Vodka." Fiona sprang from the hunter green couch. "I need alcohol. Lots of it."

Dropping his briefcase next to the couch and his jacket on the arm, he kicked out of his loafers and followed her into the kitchen. "I'm with you. I had a shitty day. You ever feel invisible?"

"Right about now? Hell yes!" She pulled out a frosty bottle of vodka from the freezer and set it on the counter. Without saying anything, Ned retrieved two glasses from the cabinet over the stove.

What a perfect roommate. They moved as a unit without a word between them. And staring at his long, slender fingers, his strong forearm and his cute, boyish, Ashton Kutcher-like looks, he was far too appealing ... and that was even before the alcohol.

She had to stop thinking about her roommate and her best friend this way. But lately everything he did, everything he touched, every time he looked at her, she wanted to jump on him, strip him out of his clothes and slide him inside of her.

If milk did a body good, then Ned must have bathed in the liquid daily since high school. The self-professed geeky kid had grown up into a tall, slightly muscled man with dreamy blue eyes she wanted to get lost in and perfect, kissable lips she longed to touch. All men should be blessed with a set like Ned's.

Probably why she kept hooking him up with different friends. If he wasn't available, she wouldn't go after him. The man used to do math problems to relax. Why would he want to be with her other than the obvious--her looks? Even though they got along, even argued like a married couple, she knew that when push came to shove he would want a woman who could match his wit. So maybe he could go for a sexy lawyer. She hoped.

"I'm trying to get this clerk's job in Judge Kristoff's court and I keep getting blown off. They won't give a sista a break." Fiona spun off the cap of the vodka bottle with one twist. She poured the clear liquid into the two glasses. After lifting them, they clinked them together.

"So why did your day suck?" Fiona asked, perching on the countertop.

Ned took a drink, tilting his head and exposing his long neck. God, it had been too long since Fiona had had a man and hard, pounding, wet, tense sex. A good fuck session.

Maybe she shouldn't have broken up with Kwame just yet. But then again, she wasn't down for staying with a man who couldn't be faithful ... no matter how badly she needed her pussy stroked. Was that why Ned seemed cuter lately? He epitomized loyalty.

"Bad meeting. My boss called me Nick."

Fiona winced. "Ouch. That's never good."

Ned shook his head, wiggling his scruffy brown hair. "I just don't stand out." He took a healthy gulp and set his glass on the counter next to Fiona, brushing his hand against her naked thigh, sending a firestorm of sparks shooting up her leg and gathering at her throbbing pussy. "What do I have to do to move up?"

Did he know what his touch did to her? Fuck, she needed a man.

"Maybe it's not what but who you have to do?" Fiona winked and tapped her leg against her friend's leg.

"I should fuck my boss, Fat Bastard?" Ned snickered. "Or maybe one of those stuck-up bitches who keep thinking I work in the mailroom instead of being a computer programmer. If they were as hot at you, it would be a no-brainer."

Fiona rolled her eyes but inside her stomach quivered. Ned thought she was hot? Maybe he needed a girlfriend. She had to set him up ... quick!

Ever since they'd met in their freshman year of high school, he'd always been quiet and reserved, but sweet. She'd recognized that when he'd walked into their beginner's French class with his head hung down, imitating a golf club, a nine iron or whichever one had the biggest head. But he was the nicest, most considerate person she'd ever met. And when their friendship had evolved, no one believed that the head cheerleader would have befriended the school nerd. But they'd clicked.

Fiona was no Freud but she figured it had a lot to do with first impressions. For example, no one thought a black head cheerleader would want to go into law. But she'd shown them, earning top grades in both college and law school. And she'd managed to convince herself that this was the dream she wanted too.

"At least you're working." Fiona finished off her drink and set the glass on the counter. "I've decided that I'm going to call my parents and tell them I'm moving back home."

Planting his hands on either sides of Fiona, trapping her in her spot on the countertop, Ned stared at her, boring his sky blue gaze into her eyes. "You are not going back home."

The intensity in his words almost made her shrink. If it hadn't been for the fact that she knew Ned had always looked out for her from the very beginning of their friendship, she would have thought his demand was more selfish than selfless.

"I can't keep sponging off of you. I'm not contributing anything to this household," she said and attempted to slide off of the counter.

Instead her legs slid around his body. Her chest pressed against his. Grabbing his arms to brace herself, Fiona's heart pounded so loud, it sounded in her ears. Her T-shirt rose up as it slid against Ned's shirt, almost exposing her bra.

Ned's breathing whispered in her ear. Without her wanting it to, her body reacted. Her shoulders relaxed, her legs squeezed him a little tighter. She clutched his arms as though she was embracing him in bed. God, what was she doing? This was her fucking roommate. Her best friend. Not the man she should fuck.

"Oh, you're doing a lot here in the house." Ned eased his hands to her hips and held her almost possessively. Did he just hook his fingers into the belt loops in her denim shorts?

She swallowed hard. Her best friend had never made her this nervous before. She needed to get laid or she needed to get a job and move out. But she wouldn't make a fool of herself by asking him out and have him laugh in her face because he couldn't take her seriously.

There were gentlemanly gestures, like opening a car door or reading a map during a road trip, that he'd performed for her whenever they'd gone out. Then there were the things she knew he did because he probably thought she couldn't handle the mental challenge. For example, Ned always demanded that he fill out their tax forms. He also ordered for her in restaurants, which wasn't bad until they went to a French restaurant and he butchered the menu items.

"What am I doing for you? Good whack-off material?" Fiona giggled but Ned cleared his throat, hitched up a nervous smile and retreated, allowing her to gain footing onto the floor.

"You cook., Hell, you're a *great* cook. You keep this place habitable so that if I had other friends, I could have company. I get cool points just being around you." He poured another drink for her then gurgled out a glass for himself.

What a gentleman. A gentle man. If he knew how much she needed him in her life, as much as he claimed he needed her, he would be charging her rent, making her change the oil in his car and demanding that she suck his cock, ride his face and fuck him on a regular basis. Wait, *maybe* those last three were items that he really wanted. They sure did top her list.

She needed to get laid.

"I'll tell you what else you do for me," he began. "You keep me sane so I don't run off and kill that fat bastard, Chunti."

Fiona's eyes widened as an idea struck. "Chunti? Your boss' name is Chunti? As in A. Frank Chunti?"

"You didn't know that?"

"You've always called him Fat Bastard." She took a sip of her drink. "Frank Chunti and Casper Kristoff are golf buddies. They host a golf tournament every year." Her mind raced with ideas. "I've got it." She downed her drink then slammed her glass on the counter. "You want to move up at work, right?"

"Among other things. I have ideas for my own software programs but without a backer or a higher title, they're just ideas." He loosened his tie and unbuttoned the top buttons of his shirt.

"I promise you that with my help, you'll get your promotion. And with you, I'll get that clerk position." Fiona smiled, finally figuring a way to fix her career dilemma and get this man into bed ... strictly as friends, of course.

"And how do you plan on doing that?" he asked.

"Dating and sex." She blurted the words as though she'd said 'education' and 'training.'

"Excuse me?"

"You are invisible at work because no one notices you, right?" She opened the menu drawer and pulled out a red-and-white take-out menu.

Ned shook his head at the menu and grimaced. Shoving it back in the drawer and retrieving a second all-yellow menu, he nodded and smiled.

"Number eight with extra noodles," he said, then handed her his wallet. "So what does dating and sex have to do with anything?"

"Gee, and I thought that naïve thing from high school was just an act."

Ned smirked. "Funny."

"Don't you know it's just like that old saying, 'It's not what you know but who you know'? You keep saying that I'm hot."

"You are."

"And you gain cool points by being around me."

"I do."

"Then this is what we're going to do. You're going to date me."

Ned's eyebrows furrowed as he stopped midway while pulling his shirttails from his pants. "Date you?"

Even confused, he looked cute.

"Just long enough for Chunti to notice and be impressed. A man with a piece of eye candy on his arm looks like a winner. And dating is a lot like getting a good job. It's all about saying and doing the right things." She picked up the phone, punched in the numbers to the take-out restaurant they both agreed on, and ordered their dinners.

"So in this dating process, will it involve..."

"Courting, dinners, parties, social appearances and sex. Lots of it. Fucking like rabbits."

Ned stared at Fiona, his mouth agape as though she'd grown a third tit. She couldn't be serious. Sure it'd been his fantasy. He'd dreamed about doing exactly what she proposed--dating her, showing her off to friends, fucking her until their bodies were rendered immobile.

But for a woman who could pass for a taller version of Jada Pinkett Smith, what would she want with a skinny white guy? Ned the Nerd? And did he really want to lose her as a friend for the sake of hot, pulse-pounding sex?

"You're crazy." He ducked into his bedroom. He should have known she would follow him.

Standing in the doorway, she folded her arms, leaned against the frame and said, "It all makes sense. I'll show up with you at company functions so people can see me. You'll look like the company stud and it'll guarantee you more interest from your bosses. They'll notice your work, and you'll get that raise and a promotion."

If she knew what the prospect was doing to him, she would have known he'd been getting a raise from her since she pressed her body against him in the kitchen. And she smelled so good. She always wore a vanilla scent that made him want to nibble every part of her body like a sugar cookie.

"And what will having sex do for my career? My ego, I know. But my career..."

"That's a no-brainer. Fucking is exactly like work. Positions. Knowing what works for your partner. Intensity. Relief."

Ned held up his hand, uncovering his growing erection. "That's enough."

Fiona pulled out a couple of twenties from his wallet for dinner and tossed the black leather billfold on his bed next to him.

"I get where you're going with this. But what will this deal do for you?"

"A nice little letter from your boss. If I can get the man alone, I can convince him to write a recommendation for me to send to Judge Kristoff. Your boss may be a slime bucket, but I bet he's got Kristoff's ear. Don't you see? This could work."

"But what about our agreement? We've remained great friends because we promised never to date and ruin our relationship."

"But this isn't sex for pleasure."

"At least with me it wouldn't be." Ned chuckled, making Fiona smile.

"This is work," she went on. "Like preparing for a job interview."

"And what makes you think I'm not sexually savvy?" he said, continuing his line of thought. He finished unbuttoning his shirt and tossed it on his dirty laundry pile in the corner of his bedroom.

"You haven't dated anyone since college, and the one girl you did date can't really be counted because, as you know, I set her up to go out with you."

And that girl was no Fiona. If Fiona knew that Ned had only dated that girl to make Fiona happy, she wouldn't see him as such the nice guy anymore.

"I think this is a great plan. We'll both get something out of it." She licked her tongue over her lips. *Why did she have to do that?* "And it won't affect our friendship. We love each other too much to let that happen. Besides, it's not like we haven't seen each other naked before."

"Yeah, you're the only woman I know who doesn't mind pissing in front of a guy."

"Hey, if I have to go, I have to go." She winked. "But don't forget that time you took care of me when I had my appendix out. You had to give me sponge baths until I could bathe myself."

Why did she have to remind him of that too? He'd remembered her sleek body, those perfect half grapefruit-sized breasts, those long legs. He wanted her. Lord knows he'd been dreaming about it for years.

"And I've taken care of you and seen you naked. Like the time you broke your leg. I had to bathe you then." She strolled over to him.

Why did she have to remind him of that time too? Ned distinctly remembered biting the insides of his cheeks, pinching his leg until he made a numb spot and even counting to a hundred in French in his head to keep from getting a hard-on when she'd bathed him.

But now she gave him the green light to pursue a physical relationship, even if it was only for a short while and fake. Maybe that was better than nothing.

It was his lust that made him answer, "Okay, you have a deal." He held out his hand to shake on the deal. Instead, she leapt on top of him, pushing him back against the bed and straddling his body.

"Lesson one starts tonight."

# *Chapter 2*

## *Realizing your dream*

The longer Fiona's body stayed on top of his, the more Ned knew she could feel his growing hard-on. How could she not? It was pressing against her stomach as she flattened her body on top of his.

"Are you sure you're not doing this because you're missing Kwame?" he asked. "Even with your room across the hall and down from mine, I could hear you two fucking all of the time without even trying. Why do you think I slept with the TV on?"

He'd hated that some other man had touched Fiona. She was his ... even if she didn't know it. But he couldn't tell her. She would laugh right in his face, call him crazy, or worse, a loser. He'd had enough of that in school from people pretending to be his friends. Fiona was the real deal.

The smile dropped from her face. "I'm such a bitch. I shouldn't have had sex here in your place, man. We should have gone to Kwame's or gotten a hotel room."

How expertly Ned had lied about the TV. Most of the time when Fiona and Kwame had had sex, Ned had listened to them intently, drowning out Kwame's voice and amplifying Fiona's. When she'd cried out for her lover, it was Ned she called. When she'd begged for more, he imagined she'd wanted it from him. And afterward, when the noise settled and all he had heard were the silent whisperings between lovers, he'd imagined himself holding Fiona, telling her he loved her and stroking her hair until they both fell asleep.

"Don't sweat it. If it had been me..."

Fiona cut him off. "You would have done the same thing."

"Slept with Kwame?"

"Sense of humor. That goes a long way in business."

"So lesson one. What does that entail?"

"I'll call it, 'Realizing Your Dream.'"

"Are you releasing this program in a book or inspirational CD? 'How to Make It Big in Business by Fucking Your Friends.'"

"Think Barnes and Noble would carry a book like that?"

"Just take out the profanity."

"Which word? 'Big' or 'business'?"

"I was thinking 'friends.'"

They both laughed, her body jiggling on top of his, causing his blood to rush through his head and lower extremities and, in particular, his swelling cock. When Fiona, looking puzzled, attempted to peer down between them, Ned grabbed her attention.

"So lesson one. 'Realizing My Dream,' which is...?"

"Um, upper management. Running your own department." She shifted higher, hovering her face over his. "You want to run your own department, right? Have a team of people under you?"

Right now he wanted Fiona under him, naked, begging him to make love to her, take her, kiss her.

He simply answered, "Yes."

"Then you need to assert some enthusiasm for that goal just like you would with a woman. So you see a woman in a bar."

"You?"

"Okay, yes, me. How do you approach me?"

Ned snickered but stopped when she didn't see Fiona sharing in his giddiness. So he comically cocked an eyebrow and said, "Hey, baby. Your feet must be tired because you've been running through my mind all night."

Fiona pursed her lips.

So Ned kept going. "If I could rearrange the alphabet, I would put 'U' and 'I' together."

She let out a long sigh.

"Heaven is missing an angel because she's down here with me."

"Stop." Fiona sprang to her feet right at the moment the doorbell rang. She paid for the food and returned to his bedroom. "Get dressed. Put on your best club outfit and meet me at Cherries."

"What?"

"You heard me. You have an hour. I put the food in the fridge and left an egg roll on a plate for you. But if you're expecting some action, you may want to hold off eating it before you go out."

"Look, I was kidding around before but we don't have to..."

"See you in an hour." She disappeared down the hall.

So much for a quiet Friday night of watching TV and talking to Fiona. Springing to his feet, he ducked into his bathroom. Time to go to work.

* ~ *

Ned could be so dumb. Why was he using those corny lines on Fiona, thinking they would work? Or maybe he knew they wouldn't work in real life, so he was making a joke out of all of this.

But this was no joke to Fiona. She needed a job. She also wanted to help her best friend so that he could feel good about himself. And she needed sex. Right now her straight-laced, clean-cut and, most importantly, disease-free friend would have to do.

He had a swimmer's body. Broad shoulders, long, lean arms, a well-muscled back and rippled abs. When did Ned the Nerd turn into Ned the Hunk?

If he hadn't turned her off with those idiotic lines, she would have had him on his bed. She'd felt his impressive, hard cock against her stomach when she'd jumped on top of him.

How could she have forgotten that God-given gift after all the times she'd bathed him when he'd broken his leg? She knew then that he wasn't attracted to her. Weeks of cleaning him and he never once got a hard-on. How could a tall drink of water like that hide something so damn good? She just hoped he didn't think she was kidding about going to Cherries.

When she'd emerged from her room after showering and dressing, she heard Ned still bustling around in his room. She'd taken that moment to head to the club.

Fiona slowly turned in her barstool when she felt a hand on her shoulder. Ah, good ol' reliable Ned. She knew he wouldn't let her down. She'd even worn her black strapless club dress with the slits up both sides, the one Ned complimented her on every time she'd worn it. Maybe that'll shake him up a little.

"Are you going to buy me a drink?" she asked. Then her mouth dropped open when she saw who it was.

Kwame. Of all of the clubs in Virginia Beach and he had to walk into hers.

She hadn't seen him in months, ever since she'd caught him cheating on her with not one but two other women ... at the same time. She knew there was a reason he didn't want to give her a copy of his apartment key. Why hadn't she figured it out?

"Still into Hennessey or have you changed?" he asked, his voice low, matching the thumping bass beats in the darkened club.

"Hi, Kwame. Bye, Kwame." She turned her back to him.

"Hold up, hold up, hold up." He said it in rapid succession so it sounded more like 'holupholupholup.' "What's this attitude? You can't give a brother no more love than that?" He spread his arms out like a regal eagle. "At least give your man a hug."

"You are not my man." She picked up her Cosmopolitan and slid off her stool.

What had she seen in him? Sure, he was too good looking for words. Great hair. Nice and curly. Great smile. Straight, white teeth. Natural, he'd told her. No braces. Golden brown skin. And tall, although Ned was a good inch or two taller.

Ned also had short, wavy chocolate brown hair. And those sweet, baby blue eyes still made her breath catch when he looked at her the right way. Maybe she didn't need to drink after all.

"Come on, girl. I know why you're here." Kwame followed her across the dance floor. Shielding her drink with one hand, she struggled to keep the pinkish liquid contained in its flared glass. It only took one bump, and she spilled some of it on a woman's foot.

Shit! The last thing she needed was a fight. But the woman immediately stopped dancing and looked down at her feet.

"These are Jimmy Choo, bitch! You're paying for these." The woman started taking off her hoop earrings.

Shit! Shit! This was *so* not Fiona's night. Her heart pounded faster than the bass beat from the music. Her stomach tightened to the size of a thimble. If her insides compressed any more, not only would the woman have her Cosmo on her shoes but also Fiona's lunch.

"I'm sorry. This asshole is bothering me," Fiona said, trying to appeal to the woman's sense of sisterhood.

"I don't give a fuck if he's O.J. These are Jimmy fucking Choo."

Why would anyone wear five hundred dollar shoes, then get upset when they got messed up while wearing them in a club with a bunch of drunks?

"So what's it going to be?" the woman asked.

Fiona opened her mouth just as Ned broke through the crowd on the dance floor. Sidling next to Fiona, he put a possessive arm around her.

Oh no. This was not the time for Nice Ned to use his logic to calm the situation down. If he wasn't careful, he was going to get hurt.

"Hey, white boy," Kwame said, his own endearing reference to Ned that Fiona hated. "Take care of this here while I take care of my woman."

"Good," Ned said, causing Fiona to damn near snap her neck when she turned to him.

What was he doing? Throwing her to the wolves?

"This gentleman will take care of your shoes." Ned addressed the other woman, then started to lead Fiona off the floor.

"Whoa. This chick ain't my woman." Kwame pointed to the shocked woman who was now taking off her rings.

"Chick? Who the hell you think you're talking to?"

"*This* woman isn't yours either. Sounds like you're having your own problems." Ned attempted to leave again, but this time Kwame grabbed the back of Ned's shirt.

"Don't you walk away from me, punk."

Ned snatched his shirt from Kwame's grip. Being manhandled didn't seem to bother him. Fiona knew he'd been bullied before by bigger guys than Kwame. It wasn't until Kwame grabbed Fiona's arm and yanked her that Ned snapped.

With lightning speed, Ned disengaged Kwame's hand from her arm with a quick, twisting motion that made Fiona's ex-boyfriend scream like a schoolgirl. Then again, not even schoolgirls whimpered that much. Then Ned did something that shocked her. He punched her ex, landing his fist right across Kwame's jaw and knocking him on his backside.

"That's for all the times you made Fiona cry." Putting his arm around her waist, Ned attempted to hustle Fiona out of the club before she got entangled any further, but he must not have accounted for Kwame's speed.

Kwame was up, at the back of his shirt again and had him turned around before Ned could put up another defense. In a flash of a disco light, Kwame landed an even bigger punch on Ned that not only knocked him on the floor but slid him across it so that he hit several dancers like a bowling ball crashing into a stack of pins.

Luckily for Ned, the people parted when they saw him throw the first punch so he didn't hit many of them. Last thing he needed was another fight he would be bound to lose.

Unluckily for him, the bouncers saw him start the fight, so they scooped him up by his collar and carried him, the way a cowboy would carry a saddle, out the front door where he was promptly thrown on his ass.

* ~ *

Once outside, Fiona crouched down, one hand on his cheek where the punch had landed and the other on his shoulder. Thank God the woman cared more for him than herself. Ned could see down her dress and caught a glimpse at the succulent curves of her breasts. That made the humiliating punch worth the trip.

"Was the fight part of the lesson?" he asked as struggled to his feet.

"Absolutely not. Kwame wasn't supposed to be a part of it either. I can't believe he still comes here." Fiona wiped the dirt from his clothes and helped him to her car, letting him drape his long arm over her shoulders. "What were you thinking back there? I've never seen you fight anyone before."

"I can't believe I just popped a guy in his eye. I've never been physically aggressive like that in my life. I guess a lifetime of being bullied came to a head. Just wish I could have had a better outcome than that."

He rubbed his face. Sparks shot through the back of his eye, making him wince. And even with the people outside still laughing at him as he strolled back to his car, he still felt like a million bucks because he had Fiona under his arm. Hey, maybe there was something about her theory of being with an incredibly good-looking woman.

"I didn't think you could get rattled like that. It makes playing basketball with you dull because you do no trash-talking." She poked him in his stomach and smiled. "At least you got through the first lesson," she said. "When obstacles come your way, you assert yourself, then get the hell out of Dodge. But next time if something like that happens to me, don't go all Rambo and try to punch the guy. It's not in you to be a jerk."

"Sounds like something that would be in Business 101." He took her keys from her hand and unlocked her car door. While holding it open, he asked, "So how did I do in my first lesson?"

"Okay."

*Okay?* Sure, Ned had gotten knocked on his ass for trying to protect her. But at least he did something. He'd gotten her out of another sticky situation. Weren't women turned on by that, by the knight-in-shining-armor deal?

Ned had even taken great pains to wear an outfit that Fiona had picked. He wore loose-fitting jeans and a pullover top that Fiona had told him all the hot rappers were wearing now. Unsure he could carry off the look, he attempted to maintain a cool demeanor.

"Good. Can we go home now?" he asked.

"Come on. It's Friday. You don't have to go to work tomorrow and the night is young."

"But there's a wonderful dinner waiting for us at home. And since you're into French movies, I rented *The Umbrellas of Cherbourg* with Catherine Deneuve." He bent over and whispered. "That's why I was so late. I stopped at the video store."

"Does that mean you got me..."

"Red licorice whips."

Wrapping her arms around his neck, Fiona kissed his throbbing cheek. He flinched and sucked in his breath.

"Oh, I'm so sorry." She gave him a light kiss on it for good measure. "You are so good to me," she said as soon as his arms went around her.

Damn. She smelled so good and her body fit his perfectly.

"Thank you." She kissed closer to his lips. "Thank you." Her mouth landed on his lips and it was over.

Fiona's head swooned, floating into the night sky as though she'd never had a head before. His lips were firm on hers, pressing down with passion, longing and urgency. Oh God, he wanted her too.

Seeing Ned all primal, protecting her like a good man should, she couldn't deny the heated wetness forming between her legs.

It didn't take long for his cock to rise again. She felt it pressing against her stomach. Ned moaned then ran his hand over her hair.

Voices behind them interrupted their passionate kiss. Some club goers were yelling things like, "Get a room" at them.

Ned blinked, looking like he hardly believed what just happened between the two of them. "I didn't mean to..."

"You didn't?" She couldn't catch her breath.

"Well..."

"Yes, you did. At least I sure as hell did."

"This is a mistake," he growled. "Maybe you should go home and I'll drive around the block a couple of times to cool off." Instead he pressed his body against hers, pinning her between the open door and the car. "Or maybe..."

Ned continued kissing her. His hands roamed her body and she felt powerless to do anything. It had been a long time since she'd had this kind of attention. It didn't help that her judgment was clouded by seeing him look so good *and* having him punch out the one man she wished she could have knocked out herself.

And his hands. God, his hands cupped her ass and squeezed, making her gasp. She lost her breath again when Ned pulled down her top and palmed her breast. His thumb rolled around her hardened nipple, begging for this kind of relief.

It was obvious from her year away from a sexual relationship that Fiona couldn't please herself the way a man could. She loved the way they touched her, the way they smelled. Right now Ned, her sweet Ned, made her trembly and breathless, not caring that she had one tit out for the world to see.

It wasn't until his hand went up her dress that Fiona snapped back into reality. As soon as his warm fingers dragged across her soaked panties, smoothing against her pussy lips and finding her clit, she broke from the embrace.

"No." She removed his hand from her breast. Her body acted as though Fiona had betrayed it. Her stomach lurched and now she felt cold. Goose bumps prickled her skin as she ducked into her car.

"What did I do wrong?" Ned asked.

Instead of answering, she replied, "See you at home." Without looking at him next to her car, she started it and drove away.

She'd wanted Ned. More than any man she'd ever been with or had ever wanted. As soon as his hand had ventured between her legs, she'd had to stop him. Thinking about what he'd said earlier about the dangers of having sex while being friends struck her immediately. Of course, he was right. Could she fuck her friend and still be friends in the morning?

* ~ *

What had he done? Why the fuck had he gone so far with Fiona? Even when she'd presented this plan and he'd agreed to it, Ned never believed he would go through with any of her crazy schemes.

But punching Kwame had given him a bigger hard-on than anything else recently, including seeing Fiona in his favorite dress of hers, the one that curved to her body in a way that

25

would make a paralyzed man walk again. He liked the feeling of being able to stand up for her even if he got knocked down in the process.

Then he went too far. How could he have continued kissing her? They were friends. They'd never kissed. Not like that. And touching her ass. No, not just touching it. Squeezing it like he was palming a basketball.

Ned pinched his eyes shut when he thought about exposing her breast and massaging it. It fit so perfectly in his hands. He needed more. He'd tried getting more when he went for her pussy.

Her sweet pussy. Ned put his fingers, the ones lucky enough to touch her soaked panties, to his nose and inhaled deeply. Her sweet scent lingered, pumping blood into his dick.

Stop it. He had to stop thinking about his friend. Yes, his *friend*, for Pete's sake. She was trying to help him and he was taking advantage of her.

* ~ *

Once at his apartment building, Ned sat in his car for fifteen minutes. He needed to let all parts of his anatomy cool before he went into the apartment. No doubt Fiona would probably be on the phone with one of her many girlfriends talking about how he'd pawed her outside of the club tonight. He shook his head. He needed a drink. Now.

He opened the door to the apartment. Eerily quiet wasn't close to describing the silence he encountered. And he didn't see or hear Fiona. Good. Maybe she was asleep. Or maybe she was just avoiding him. Either way, he didn't have to worry about any confrontation.

He strolled into the kitchen and nuked a plate of the Chinese food delivered earlier. Since he couldn't satisfy his appetite for sex, food would have to do.

With a plate in one hand and a can of root beer in the other, Ned tiptoed to his room, careful not to wake Fiona. But as soon as he stepped into his room he realized it didn't matter. Sitting on his bed wearing his T-shirt and nothing else was Fiona.

"What took you so long?"

# *Chapter 3*

## *Working with what you have*

Ned looked as confused as Fiona had been just an hour before. When she'd gotten home in lightning speed, she quickly realized the monster she'd released by coming up with this plan to enhance Ned's career via sex. Sounded good at the time. But now she wasn't so sure she could go through with it.

Sitting on his bed covered with a dark blue comforter, she wondered what he must have thought. He probably thought she'd just stepped out of the loony bin and had forgotten to take her medication. So she sucked in a deep breath and tried hard to look composed and in control ... even though her insides were doing a double back handspring.

"I thought you weren't coming home," she said.

"Actually I did think about getting a hotel room for the night." He strolled across the room and sat at his computer desk.

Just the sound of his deep voice got her juices flowing. Her clit throbbed as though Ned's voice and body were the keys to unlocking her pleasure. She would have stood, but her legs felt powerless. Her clitoris throbbed in sync with her pounding heart.

"I'm glad you didn't. You know I hate sleeping in this apartment by myself." She chuckled, trying to lighten the mood but Ned wasn't having it. He popped open his soda, making the can hiss, then he dove into his food.

Watching him, Fiona felt her nipples get hard. What was it about him that drove her crazy? They were friends. They'd watched countless movies together. He'd painted her toenails when she'd hurt her hand playing softball. He'd been there when Kwame had broken her heart.

Although there was nothing like Ned's touch, Fiona couldn't help herself when she'd gotten home after the parking lot fiasco. She'd stripped off her clothes and hopped into the shower hoping to wash away all sexually motivated thoughts. Instead, as her hands roamed her body, cascading over her swollen tits and easing down between her legs, she found comfort in masturbating to satisfaction.

She'd squeezed her nipple, rolling it between her thumb and index finger until she felt her body teetering on the brink of an orgasm. But she knew that wasn't enough. Her fingers stroked her pussy lips as the heel of her hand rubbed against her clit. But the moment wouldn't be complete without thinking of the perfect man. The one man who could make her come.

Ned. As soon as the image of his face hit her thoughts, Fiona's body had shaken uncontrollably. Slipping a finger inside the swollen walls of her pussy while resting her foot on the side of the tub, she pounded her own vagina, moving her finger in and out until that wasn't enough. She slid a second finger inside, which made her howl. Secretly she wished he had come home now to really finish her off. Would he have given her another leg-trembling kiss?

His last girlfriend, the one Fiona had set him up with, must have been crazy for saying Ned couldn't kiss and was lousy in bed. Ned had used his tongue like an artist. She couldn't imagine what he was like with his penis.

"It's my fault," Fiona said.

That made Ned stop his fork halfway to his mouth and stare at her with disbelief.

"I give you this plan but then I don't set any of the ground rules. Rule number one is that we shouldn't kiss. It complicates things." At least in her mind it did.

"But sex wouldn't?" He finished off his plate of food and his soda in seemingly three hefty gulps. "Fi, it was a nice try." He stood and picked up his plate. "I'll figure out something on my own at work. Maybe I need to be personable."

She let out a long breath, stood and sauntered by him. His room smelled like a combination of them: the cologne she'd given him for Christmas with a hint of practicality that smelled like a mix between Lysol and Speed Stick. The scent swirled around her as she moved. Her gaze met his as they both stood in the doorway.

"How are you going to change to Mr. Personality if you're already running away from your friends?" She disappeared into her room, closing her door behind her.

* ~ *

Running away? Hell, he was being a gentleman. After depositing his plate in the kitchen with the thought of cleaning it in the morning, Ned stomped by Fiona's door, looking at it as though she were right there watching him.

He couldn't resist responding to her last question. "Friends don't give friends blue balls!"

With that, he stormed into his room and topped off the comment with a door slam. He stripped out of his clothes. Even though he'd taken a shower before heading out to the club, he needed another, one slightly cooler. A lot cooler.

Ducking into the shower, he let the icy pellets hit the top of his head and cascade down his back. The cold made him shake and caused his stomach and lungs to crunch themselves into compact balls. The frigid water turned his overheated body into a tall, lanky Popsicle. But at least it got his mind off of Fiona's body.

Closing his eyes, his mind immediately brought up the image of Fiona in that dress. Her nipples jutted out so far it looked like she'd had two pebbles under her top. If he hadn't touched one himself, he would have sworn the woman had had some cosmetic surgery. They were far too firm and round to be real. But now he had proof. Real, honest-to-God proof. Her tits were real.

And her legs. Those long, luscious, toned legs that he wanted her to wrap around his body. And that ass.

He couldn't resist. Grabbing the base of his now hardened cock, Ned eased his hand up and down the length, paying special attention to the sensitive tip. He leaned his head back and braced his other hand against the wall.

Tightening his grip, he imagined the sensation to match what he would experience inside of Fiona. He stroked himself faster and faster. The trembling he'd experienced from the initial icy shower continued but this time because of his building orgasm. Now he couldn't get the water cold enough to douse his heated flesh.

Moans rattled in his throat until Fiona's name came through his lips. With quivering legs, he constricted his grip and stroked himself with the passion he wanted to use to fuck Fiona.

He could imagine her on top of him like she was earlier this evening. She would want to take control because that was Fi. Her way or the highway. That was one of the things that Ned liked about her. Loved, actually. He could see her tits bouncing up and down while she was on top, riding him hard until they both collapsed into a pool of sweat and sex and flesh.

Feeling the lust build inside of him, Ned released a long growl along with his semen all over the shower stall wall. He sighed and slid down the back wall.

He couldn't live like this. It was bad enough living with Fiona when she didn't know he wanted to have sex with her. Now that she did, how would she be around him now? Would she want to move or stay with him?

* ~ *

It was the first time in years Ned didn't mind going in to work on a Monday. The weekend proved to be long and awkward with Fiona and Ned barely exchanging two words.

Harmless bumps and brushes had caused a shower of apologies, whereas before they would have just understood it was a mistake or not big enough to comment on or, better yet, made a joke about it.

Except for that first day of high school when he didn't know anyone, this was the first time he had ever felt so uncomfortable around her. The unease turned his stomach and gave him a pounding headache that wouldn't go away no matter how much ibuprofen he swallowed.

What hurt the most was having Fiona avoid all eye contact. He missed staring into her soft green eyes. He didn't know what he had to do to gain her trust back, but he had to figure it out fast. He couldn't lose his best friend.

Walking to his workstation, Ned noticed the strange stares from his coworkers. He was used to the little office cliques clucking their tongues and giggling as he walked by. But there seemed to be something different in the whispers today.

The women weren't laughing; they were smiling. The men nodded their heads. Ned patted his pants pocket to make sure he didn't have the winning lottery ticket hanging out. And in one easy swoop, he brushed his front fly to make sure his zipper wasn't down.

Milliseconds after sitting down, Too Much Perfume glided over to him, surrounding him with a strange, antiseptic concoction she must have thought smelled good in either the store or in her house or in her car. Wherever. It didn't work.

"Here are the updates on that new program you're working on." She handed him a CD but lingered over him with a goofy smile.

"Uh, thanks," he said, trying to get rid of her by turning to face his computer screen.

"No problem, tough man." When he looked up in surprise, she winked before walking away.

*Tough man?* What was that about? His face and eye hadn't swelled as much as he thought it would after the punch. It wasn't as if he'd come to work with a black eye and cut lip.

Nose-Picker approached next, giving Ned a playful punch in his arm and then feigned fear by tripping back. "Don't want you knocking me out."

*Oh God.* His coworkers had somehow heard about him punching Kwame. He wasn't particularly proud of having to resort to his fists, but the moment had seemed right. Whoever saw the fight, though, must not have stayed until the end when he'd gotten decked and thrown out on his ass. Not exactly his shining moment.

"Look, let me explain about that."

"No need to explain." Nose-Picker closed in to Ned's personal space. "And I heard you walked out with a real looker too. Did you tap that ass?"

So the spectator *had* stayed for the whole fight. And it seemed that what mattered most was the eye candy he'd walked out with and not that he'd lost the fight.

As much as he appreciated the attention, he hated to have an asshole like this talk about Fiona that way. She wasn't a piece of meat. She was his friend.

To disarm the man, Ned asked, "What's my name?"

Nose-Picker blinked. "What, are you still drunk from Friday night or something?"

"Seeing as we've never had a conversation before I got into a fight and walked off with a beautiful woman, I just wanted to know if you even know me well enough to tell you anything about my personal life. If you can tell me my name," he said, flipping his I.D. badge over, "without looking at my badge or my nameplate in my cubicle, I'll tell you every dirty detail of what happened that night."

Nose-Picker laughed nervously, wiped the back of his neck with his hand and shook his head. "You're funny, man." He rubbed his nose.

It wouldn't take the fucker long to probe his finger in one of his thin nostrils. Without confirming what Ned already knew, his coworker walked away without saying Ned's name.

At least Fiona had been right about one thing, having her by his side got people to notice him. He let out a long breath before settling in to work. That was before he got another visitor.

Mr. Chunti.

His boss pointed his chubby finger at him and said with conviction, "Nolan."

Ned pointed back at Fat Bastard and said, "Ned."

"Oh, I knew it began with an 'N.'"

"At least you were in the ballpark." Ned hoped the man wouldn't catch on to his sarcasm. From the way he barreled on to the topic at hand, Ned guessed the windbag hadn't.

"I have a Fourth of July picnic at my house in Sandbridge every year. Only the V.P.'s and their significant others are invited. I'd like you to come. It's this Saturday. My secretary should be forwarding you the information on directions, dress code and any other pertinent items some time this week."

"But you barely know my name. Why would you invite me to your home?" The question came out faster than Ned could stop himself, but he had to know.

Mr. Chunti scrunched his face into a tight ball, which substituted for a genuine smile, then said, "Because I think big things are going to happen for you. Any man who protects his property is all right with me."

*Property?* Ned wanted to throw up right on Fat Bastard's shoes. Fiona was no one's property. Certainly not his.

"Just be sure to bring a date with you." Mr. Chunti winked and waddled away.

A date. Chunti wasn't interested in him. He wanted Fiona. He wanted to see just who he'd protected on Friday night. Obviously whoever it was from his job who'd seen him that night spread the word that not only did he kick some ass but he'd thrown Fiona over his shoulder like a bounty and fucked her in the parking lot. Was anyone sane anymore?

The voice of Clint Eastwood saying 'Go ahead. Make my day.' came from his computer speakers and broke his concentration. He had a new e-mail. Surprise, surprise. It was from Fat Bastard's secretary. The e-mail couldn't be forwarded, printed, or replied to. He was surprised Chunti hadn't figured out a way to have it disappear ten seconds after opening it.

Fuck him. The man barely knew his name but suddenly wanted him at his house to share shitty cucumber sandwiches with his yes-men. His hand hovered over the delete command on the e-mail until he remembered Fiona. She'd wanted a letter. And the way Chunti drooled over the thought of her, she was sure to get the letter and anything else she wanted if she asked.

He shuddered knowing that. And although his first impulse was to not tell Fiona about the invitation, he decided a deal was a deal. If she wanted to go, he would go. She would be proud to know that lesson one translated nicely. Realize your dream.

# *Chapter 4*

### *Don't accept the first deal*

Ned had masturbated while thinking of her. The thought still brought Fiona up short. Friday night after he'd screamed through her door that she'd given him blue balls, she'd thought about his words and let them bounce around in her head before deciding to storm into his room and give him a piece of her mind.

She wasn't being a tease. She was just caught up in a moment. They were supposed to be pretend dating. Not for real, but as practice. Did Ned really think she would fuck him on a first date? Then again, she had fucked Kwame on their first date. Probably why their relationship didn't work.

But Ned was different. They'd known each other for twelve years, almost half of their lives. It wasn't really a first date no matter how she'd rationalized it to herself. It was a continuation of what had been bubbling inside both of them, the lusty need to take one another.

So when she watched Ned stroking his long, hard cock and calling out her name through his clear shower curtain decorated with cats and dogs, Fiona's knees had nearly given out. She'd almost collapsed to the floor. Had it not been for the overpowering need to watch him come, she would have run back to her room.

How she'd managed not to say anything to him over the weekend surprised her. No matter what kind of argument they'd had, they'd always made up with each other the same day. This time it was different. Things had changed and she hated it. This must have been what Ned had meant about sex and friendship. But, like always, she would prove her dear friend wrong.

Stirring pasta in a steaming pot on the stove, she snapped out of her trance when the front door slammed. Ned's slight smile meant he had something to say and wasn't sure how she would take it. She mentally sighed. Years of knowing him and she knew his every facial expression and mood.

"Pat yourself on the back, honey," he began. "You were right."

When Fiona established the spaghetti noodles were cooked to her satisfaction, she turned off the stove burner. "Right about what?"

"Someone from work saw my little altercation with Kwame and watched you and me walk out together." Ned took off his tie and unbuttoned his shirt. From the way he shifted from one side to the other, she knew he'd removed his shoes.

"Really? So what happened?" She poured the hot water and pasta into a colander, allowing the steam to hit her face and open her pores. If she had to do things on a budget, she could consider this her spa facial.

"I got invited to my boss' Fourth of July party in Sandbridge. Well, actually *we* got invited."

"What do you mean, 'we'? Those people don't know me."

"You're right. Whoever it was that saw me at Cherries thinks you're my girlfriend, or as my boss puts it, 'my property.' " He shivered and grimaced.

Fiona wanted to kiss him right there and then.

"I may have doubted you, Fi, but you were right. People were talking to me today who I'd never seen before in my life. It was like I was Mike Tyson and I had the championship belt."

"Hmm, go with Lennox Lewis or Roy Jones, Jr. Mike is a little too crazy to be comparing yourself to him."

"Point taken. But don't you see? You were right. It's all going to work out. I'll get promoted. And forget about Fat Bastard writing you a glowing letter. You can meet Kristoff in person. And we don't have to have sex."

Fiona shook out the colander and sighed. "But you know we have to do something, right?"

She poured the noodles into a large ceramic bowl and set it on the breakfast bar in front of Ned, now with a comically confused expression on his face.

She had thought about their situation all weekend. They needed to have sex. Fuck. Get it out of their systems. Otherwise they would always wonder, *what if*? But they didn't have to do it all right away. Baby steps. Just like dating.

"What do you mean? They already think we're a couple."

"Yeah, but you and I don't think that way, nor do we act that way, and in order to fool your coworkers and especially your boss, we're going to have to break down some barriers and establish some intimacy."

"Sounds like some lawyer doubletalk to me." Ned whipped the tie through his collar and lumbered down the hall to his bedroom.

But Fiona wasn't done talking. She rushed down the hallway, pushing his door open. Ned already had his shirt and

T-shirt off and was undoing his pants when Fiona planted herself on his bed. Used to be that Ned had no problems taking off his pants in front of her. This time he hesitated.

Seeing him watch her cautiously felt like a punch in her gut. Trust was the one thing she could count on with him. If they didn't have that, they had nothing.

Her stomach wrenched again when she thought about revealing the truth. But if she wasn't able to admit how she really felt about going into law, then how could she explain it to him? Ned enjoyed her cooking but could he understand that she wanted it to be more than a hobby to her?

"If we held hands at the party, would that make you feel weird?" she asked.

He snorted. "Of course not. You're my best friend."

"Okay, how about if we kissed? Or if you wanted to playfully slap my ass? Or if I wanted to simulate a blow job with a hot dog?"

Ned's eyes widened. "You would do that?"

"Point is if I did, you can't have that expression." She pointed to his face, which made him peep at his reflection in his dresser mirror. "You've got to act like everything I do we've done before. We're supposed to be a *couple*."

"A couple of what? Ha, ha."

She stood up and sauntered over to him, staking herself in front of him like a totem pole. "A couple without hang-ups or issues."

"Find me a couple like that and you should put them on display for the world to see."

His wiry but muscled chest and stomach tempted her to drag her tongue over him. But she held back. It didn't help that his heavy-lidded expression defined the phrase 'bedroom eyes.'

Ned strained a swallow then asked, "And how are we going to pretend to be a happy couple?"

"You'll have to know everything about me."

"I do. I know your favorite color. Blue."

"Like your eyes."

Ned blushed. "I know your favorite drink. A dirty martini without the olive. I know that you cry at the end of *The Color Purple* even if you missed the beginning of the movie. I know you hate thunderstorms. I know your first pet, a cat, was named Le Bon after Simon Le Bon of Duran Duran."

"But do you know what turns me on?"

"Besides the law?"

"Yes."

"Should I?"

God, maybe he was lousy in the sack like his last girlfriend had said. Any man who didn't want to know what turned his woman on in bed was either selfish or inexperienced. Poor Ned.

She didn't answer. He would have to figure it out. Since his forte was solving puzzles and riddles, she knew this bait was too much for him to pass up.

Instead he shook his head. "I've seen this movie before and read this book a thousand times." He finally took off his pants. "We have sex. It's great."

"Humble much?"

He picked up his black-and-white checkered pajama pants, the ones Fiona had gotten him for his birthday, and slipped them on. Without looking at her or acknowledging her sarcastic statement, he continued, "Okay, fine. So it starts off bad. I'm a horrible lover or maybe we're just too clumsy together. But I know you, Fi. You're the type who will say, 'Come on. Let's roll up our sleeves and keep trying 'til it's right.' It gets too good for us and the lines get blurred."

He tied off the drawstrings at his waist so tight Fiona was afraid he'd cut himself off at it.

Why was he so determined not to do this? He wanted her. She knew that. And now he knew she wanted him. It was a no-brainer.

"I love you, Fi. There's nothing I wouldn't do for you. But sex between us won't work. I don't care if the key to getting promoted lies in between your thighs. If the choice is between option A making love to you, getting promoted but losing you in the process, or option B not making love to you and being miserable at work but still having our friendship, I'm going with option B. I can live in misery as long as I have you."

Her mouth hung open. As soon as she got her thoughts about her, she said, "Very romantic. You should use that line when you propose to your future wife."

He gazed at her hard while heading for the door. "I'll remember that. Now come on. Pasta's getting cold."

That wasn't all that had gone cold.

# *Chapter 5*

### *Learn to compromise*

That little speech he'd given Fiona had to have been the hardest thing Ned had ever said. Mainly because although he'd meant every word of it, his body couldn't deny that it still wanted her. And Fiona was a smart woman. She could tell from the way he hadn't looked at her throughout dinner that there was still something wrong.

"Are we okay?" she'd asked at the end of the meal.

He'd chuckled like she was crazy but still couldn't look at her. "Of course, we're fine." Then he'd gathered their plates and did the dishes.

"Funny. I thought friends could look each other in the eyes. My mistake." With that statement, Fiona had kept herself locked in her bedroom the rest of the night.

He'd stood outside her door for several minutes, wanting to say something. Anything.

Instead he'd said what they usually said to each other at the end of the day, "Love you like a rock." It was a lyric from an old Paul Simon song that his parents once made Fiona listen to when she'd come by after school to help Ned with his French homework. He could still remember his dad dancing around their stuck-in-the-sixties den complete with an orange and green vinyl couch, wood paneling on the walls, rabbit ears on the TV, and white, orange and green shag carpet.

After his dad had finished his dance and established, in his own mind, that he was the hippest father in the neighborhood even though he'd played a then-twenty-year-old song and danced around like an idiot, Ned and Fiona couldn't stop laughing.

So that was how they said good-bye to each other. One always said "Love you like a rock" and the other invariably laughed without fail.

But this time there was no laughter. He heard nothing inside of her room. Maybe she was asleep already. Ned padded to his room, closed his door behind him, turned on his TV and plopped into bed. He should have been working on his program but his heart wasn't in it.

Flipping the channels, he stopped momentarily when he caught Jada Pinkett Smith in a movie where she was a bank robber or something. Right now though she was on a date ... and looking exactly like Fiona. Same green eyes. Same sharp cheekbones. Same buttery smooth complexion. Same bright smile, framed by the fullest lips he'd ever seen, lips he'd gotten to touch once.

God, Fiona defined beautiful. And she was right down the hall and wanted to have sex with him. Of course it was under the guise of business promotion, but who cared. She'd offered and he had turned her down flat. He had to be the stupidest man on the planet.

He stared at Jada's character as she moved across the screen. As much as the male actor Ned had seen before but whose name he didn't remember had wanted to protect her character, Ned felt the same for Fiona.

But if he were honest with himself and with Fiona, he would have told her the truth. He didn't want to have sex with her because he wanted her to want him. Pure and simple. He didn't want her doing him a favor or having sex with him out of pity, but because of genuine want. Tall order, he knew. But he wasn't about to buckle.

At a gun shot in the movie, a thundering crack sounded outside, blinking the lights in his room and causing Ned to flinch.

"Damn. I really wanted to watch the rest of this flick too." He clicked off the TV and set the remote on the nightstand next to him. Then he picked up a book, a mystery with a not-so-savvy detective and his gorgeous assistant. Ah, life was never as strange as fiction. If that were the case, Fiona would be in his bed right now.

A flash of lightning lit up his room and approximately five Mississippis later the thunder crashed. He still counted out in his head the number of seconds between lightning and thunder, a trick he'd done since he was six. It all fascinated him then. He felt like if he could count the seconds between the lightning and thunder then he was in some sort of control.

Another flash popped.

"One Mississippi. Two Mississippi." Before he got to three, thunder rumbled the apartment and the lights went off. "Damn." He tossed his book toward his nightstand was and knocked the remote control to the floor. "Fuck!"

He had to get to his flashlight in the closet. If Fiona woke up to find no power, she would freak.

As he crawled to the edge of his bed he heard a thump outside of his door, kind of like someone ran into it. Then came the frantic clawing and knocking.

"Ned! Ned! The power's off!" Fiona screamed.

Making his way through the darkness while trying to get his eyes to adjust, he made it to the door, opened it and got a whole-body tackle when she ran into him, throwing her arms around his neck and trembling. The only thing he saw was her white camisole and white bikini panties, which glowed against her honey-colored skin thanks in part to the spare moonlight that filtered through his blinds.

"It's okay." He stroked her back as he led her to his bed. He'd been through this before with her. The only way she could calm down would be to lie in bed with him while he held her. Amazing. She still hadn't grown out of hating thunderstorms no matter what Ned had said about them to ease her fears.

Feeling his way to his bed, he plopped down, pulling Fiona with him. She wasn't about to let him go.

"I tried to be strong," she said, her voice vibrating with fear. "I wasn't going to come in here at all."

"It's okay. I know this scares you." He covered them in his comforter although he knew without any power they were going to be sweating pretty soon.

"Th-th-then the power went off."

"Let me see if it's out all over or just us. It could be a tripped breaker." Ned was about to let her go to look out of the window but she tightened her hold.

"No! Don't leave me! I don't care if anyone else is off. Just hold me."

"But if it's just us, I could get the lights on now. And if it's the whole building, I should report it to get the power company out here."

"Please," was all she said as her body rippled with small tremors. He'd never seen her this frightened before.

After kissing her on top of her forehead, he rubbed his hand over her back. "Okay. I won't go. We'll stay right here." Although he kept his arms against her, he lifted his hands to set the alarm on his watch.

"What are you doing?" she asked, mild irritation lacing her voice.

"If we're going to be without power all night, I have to set some alarm to wake up in the morning. Can't be late for work."

She snuggled closer to him, wrapping her leg around his and pressing her chest against him. Damn, that all felt too good.

Stop it, asshole. You're supposed to be comforting your friend, not getting a boner!

Putting his arms back around Fiona and making small circles on her back, Ned let out a long breath and tried hard to concentrate on something other than this hot woman who needed him.

"You want to talk?" he asked.

Sometimes she liked that. She'd start babbling about her childhood or past boyfriends or about her favorite TV shows. Basically anything to keep her mind off of the light-and-boomer show outside.

He felt her head move but couldn't tell if it was a nod or if she was shaking her head. So he took a chance.

"I'm reading a really good book now. No sex. All action and mystery."

After sniffing, she said in a small voice, "Yeah?"

Relief waved over him. He smiled. "Yeah. The hero reminds me of that crazy uncle of yours, the one with all the cats."

"Rupert."

"Yeah. Tall, skinny black guy. Gold tooth in the front, Afro and a hoop earring."

"Yep, that's Uncle Rupert all right." She giggled and wiped her hand over her face. In the darkness he couldn't tell if she was wiping away tears or just rubbing her eyes.

"But he's got this sexy assistant. Ginger or Sugar or Cinnamon. Some spice."

"You don't know her name?"

"I can't remember the main character's name. You know I'm not good with names. I just remember that her name was something you got out of the kitchen. A spice or something."

Fiona laughed. When she looked up, his sight had finally adjusted to the darkness and he saw the whites of her eyes. Then a lightning flash brightened the room and made her eyes widen in horror before the thunder clapped. She curled her body into a ball then repositioned herself with her knees now under his armpit, her face under his chin and her chest flat against his.

That at least solved one problem. With his growing erection he was afraid her leg would bump it and cause a whole lot of questions. He rested one hand on her hip and the other stroked her hair.

"I hate the summertime in Virginia Beach," she said. "You can't go down to the beach because of all the fucking tourists. Then there are the thunderstorms. And if that wasn't enough, we have hurricane season right after that. We need to move, Ned. Get out of this place."

"What, you think the thunderstorms and hurricanes are targeting this apartment complex?" He laughed and that made her body go tight.

"No. We need to leave Virginia. Go someplace warm like Florida."

"They have worse hurricanes than us."

"California."

"Earthquakes and brush fires."

"Hawaii."

"Volcanoes."

"I don't know. Jamaica."

"You want to work as an attorney in Jamaica?" Ned thought about it for a while and a smile crept up. "Yeah, I can see it. You in a white string bikini, trying a case. Then when you win, the whole courtroom will go into a limbo contest. How low can you go? How low can you go?"

This time when he laughed, she laughed with him.

"You are not funny," she said between giggles.

"And yet you're laughing."

She brought her gaze up to meet his. The moonlight between the slats of his window blinds highlighted her green eyes perfectly. He hoped she couldn't feel his heartbeat speed up but from the way she held him tighter, he figured she must have sensed a change in mood.

"I hate it when we fight." She pressed her chin into his chest, making her lips just inches away from his.

"Me, too."

She took a deep breath then blurted, "I'm so fucking horny, Ned. That's why I came up with that plan."

His heart settled a bit. Not what he'd wanted to hear but the one thing he could always count on with Fiona was honesty. He'd always appreciated that.

"I'm sorry," she continued. "I never wanted to use you. I thought it would be okay. We're friends. We know neither one of us would hurt the other. I know you're clean. I know I'm clean. I got tested every month after I dumped Kwame."

"I know." He remembered how nervous she'd been every month when she'd gotten tested.

"And I thought since I was allowing myself to get used..." She trailed off unable to complete the statement. "Can you forgive me? I'm a horrible friend."

"No you're not." He kissed her temple. "Truth be told, I struggled with wanting to go through with it for that same reason. I wanted you so much but I didn't want our friendship to suffer. I don't have a lot, but our friendship means more to me than anything in the world. You know that, right?"

"Of course. Just like with me. I would die for you." She gave him a quick peck on the lips. Then he heard her swallow hard. She kissed him again, a little longer this time. His hand that rested on her hip squeezed it gently.

Fiona's breathing increased. Her breaths matched the pounding rain outside, hitting against his window. Listening to her and holding her, Ned's heart started a crazy, hammering rhythm.

"Fi," he said in a short breath.

Instead of responding verbally, Fiona kissed him harder. His tongue slid into her hot mouth. She sucked it like he'd imagined her taking his penis in her mouth. When she moaned, it not only vibrated his tongue but also his lips and body.

His hand cupped the back of her head as his other hand smoothed over her firm ass. He had never forgotten how absolutely perfect her backside was when he'd squeezed it the other night outside of the club.

One of Fiona's hands clutched his shoulder while the other hand danced down the side of his body, eventually reaching the waistband of his pajama pants. Just the proximity of her hand stirred his engorged penis, making it throb even more. As though she read his thoughts, her hand gently swept over his cock.

His breath caught as she pulled from him.

She said, "We don't have to, well, you know..."

"Yeah." Ned nodded, knowing exactly what she was going to say.

"Not all the way."

"Exactly."

"We would be each other's..."

"Relief."

She sighed. "Yeah. Relief."

Without another word, Ned stripped off her top and tossed it to the floor. Fiona made short work of undoing his pajamas as they both pulled them and his boxer briefs down in one tug.

"We'll still be friends," Fiona said with a lilt of questioning in her voice.

"Damn right." He yanked off her panties, nearly tearing them in the process. "Friends with benefits."

Thunder boomed as he rolled her on her back and kissed her. He never thought kissing could be this erotic. But having Fiona's full lips touch his, he was in heaven. Her soft lips tasted sweet, like strawberries dipped in honey. Here he had every straight man's dream in his bed and it was him she wanted.

Moving down her neck, laving her warm flesh in kisses along the way, he sucked a nipple into his mouth. His body shook when she moaned in reaction. She smelled of a sexy bakery. Vanilla and sugar with a hint of a womanly aroma. Her fingers dove into his hair, grabbing it, mussing it, as he took no mercy on her pebble-hard nipple.

Ned was exactly what Fiona needed, what she wanted. As she suspected, his long fingers felt amazing against her skin, massaging one breast while he continued suckling at the other. His mouth reluctantly pulled from her one tit. Dragging his tongue across her hot, tingling skin, he quickly latched on to her other nipple.

Lessons? Ned was teaching her a thing or two.

For a man with such a boyish face and charm about him, he smelled so good. So manly. It was a great combination of the cologne she'd gotten him for Christmas with his own essence. He smelled musky and playful and powerful all at once. Just taking his aroma in made her wetter, made her clit throb even more. She arched her back.

She had already broken a sweat. His hand slipped down and underneath her body to cup her ass. He was so hot. When she ran her fingers through his hair, it felt damp.

"Too hot," he murmured.

Before she could stop him, he leapt from the bed. He hoisted the blinds up and threw open his window, allowing the cool storm breeze to flow in. The cool air hit her skin and it felt incredible. She couldn't wait for Ned to return to bed.

Moonlight cascaded over his body, spotlighting his muscled torso and his fully erect and very impressive dick. Damn, not even Kwame was as big as Ned. She wasn't about to let an opportunity to please Ned go to waste.

When he stepped to the side of the bed, Fiona sat in front of him, facing his erection. His body twitched when she wrapped her fingers around his shaft.

"I wish I could see your face, look into your eyes," he moaned.

She responded by licking his bulbous tip. His sweet but salty pre-cum bubbled at the tip. After releasing a long moan, his hand dove into her short hair. Wrapping her legs around him, she pulled him in closer. In one easy motion, she took him all in and held him in her mouth while a string of profanities dripped from his mouth.

Curving her tongue around his thick shaft while cupping his tight balls, she moved her mouth up and down on him, faster and faster until she felt him moving back and forth, fucking her mouth. His legs trembled between hers and it reminded her of the way she'd just quivered only moments before when he'd comforted her.

As she stroked his shaft and massaged his balls, her tongue pressed against the tip, releasing more of his juices. Just when she thought he was about to explode, Ned pulled back from her.

"You're getting me too close, baby. I want you to come first," he said breathlessly.

Easing her back onto the bed and positioning her so that her head rested comfortably on the pillows, Ned crawled between her legs. Fiona's stomach tightened into a knot anticipating what he would do next. What he did made her want to crawl out of her skin.

He first kissed down her inner thighs. His kisses, each precise and deliberate, were so slow that they made her writhe in both agony and ecstasy. As he kissed his way down her legs, he would follow by lightly blowing on her skin, intensifying the feeling even more.

Rubbing her feet back and forth on the bed while grabbing the posts on the headboard did nothing to calm her. She wanted his hot mouth on her pussy and she wanted it now. Instead, he cranked up the torture by gently blowing on her pulsating clit as though igniting a slow-burning campfire.

"Ned, please," she said between gritted teeth.

"What? Say it."

"I want you to lick it." She tried wrapping her legs around his head to give him a hint but Ned was an expert at this game. He pried her legs apart and held them there until he got his desired response.

"Tell me exactly what you need me to do," he said, baiting her.

Lifting her head from the pillows, she screamed, "I want you to eat my pussy, Ned. I want your mouth on me. I want your tongue inside of me. Make me come."

"That's all you had to say."

53

She thought she saw him wink at her. He dove down, his mouth covering her clitoris. She released a scream so loud she was afraid the neighbors would call the police thinking Ned was chopping her body into small bits. Had they known he was giving her the best head ever, they would probably want to watch.

He spread her lower lips apart and with a flick of his tongue, teased her swollen clit until she was a quivering mess. Her head fell back on the pillows as she squeezed her eyes shut and drowned in the pleasure. As though he had done it a million and one times on her before, he sucked her clit while his hands massaged her inner thighs.

A fire burned inside of Fiona, a fire she'd tried controlling by deep breathing, then by grabbing the back of Ned's head. Her other hand balled into a fist and her legs closed around his head as the excitement built inside of her. With a final stroke of his probing tongue, he managed to do what most men in her life had not: gotten her to orgasm through oral sex.

"Damn it, Ned! Ned! Ned! Fuck!" Her knotted stomach released, relaxing as the wave of her orgasm flowed through her body, down her legs, through her fingertips and from her sweet, hot center. She couldn't tell if the flash that blinded her came from the lightning or if it resulted from the intense orgasm.

But instead of stopping and savoring the moment, he moved down her tight pussy and slipped his tongue into her opening. With only a few probes inside of her, she came even faster than when he'd sucked her clitoris. Who was this man and what had he done with Nice Ned?

Moving up to meet her gaze, Ned positioned himself next to her and crushed her mouth with his. She tasted her sex on his mouth and wasn't offended by it or his kiss.

So enthralled by the feel of his lips, she didn't notice his hand creeping down her body until it rested at her swollen pussy with its landing strip of hair.

"I wish this were real," he growled in her ear as his fingers smoothed down her puffy labia lips.

"It is." Pulling his head down, she smothered her lips over his. She'd forgotten--nor would she have cared--about her rule of not kissing.

Ned slid his long middle finger inside of her, making her gasp. She clamped her tight pussy walls around his finger as he moved it in and out of her. Her body writhed in slow motion.

As he increased the speed of his pumping finger, the intensity heightened.

"Faster," Fiona demanded. "Harder. I need to come, baby."

The muscles in her legs ached from holding their spread open position. Ned slid another finger inside, bolting Fiona upright. She draped one leg over his, then thrust her hips up and down to meet his fingers. Juices dripped from her, sliding between her cheeks. He pumped faster and faster.

She was ready. More than ready. The only thing that would make this experience better would be to see his face, watch him watch her come over and over again.

With loud, fierce passion, Fiona came again. Her body quivered into a mass as she relaxed on the bed. Ned slowed the piston motion of his fingers, finally sliding them out of her.

Ned brought his arm over her body to hold her. But Fiona had a plan of her own. She shoved his shoulders back on the bed then straddled him. In a possessive grab, she held the shaft of his cock, sliding her hand up and down it.

"I have to have you," she said.

They'd promised. As much as she wanted to keep their friendship, she couldn't stop her body from seeking what it needed.

"I'm on the pill." She rubbed the tip of his enlarged penis over her wet opening.

Ned asked, "What about what we just promised?"

Fiona didn't want to answer the question.

"I trust you," she said. She slipped just the head inside of her and released a small cry, a relieved cry like she'd been looking forward to this moment for all of her life.

"Baby, wait." He held onto her thighs. Before she could lower herself any further, the lights in his room flashed on.

She stared at her best friend as she froze on the spot. His clear blue eyes were now dark. And just like his alarm clock that now flashed twelve o'clock, it seemed like everything in that room had started over again, too. Gazing down at their union, she ran her tongue over her lips and whispered a curse.

Fuck! Damn efficient power company. Why couldn't they have waited five more minutes?

Fiona broke her gaze as she raised herself off of Ned's cock but didn't release him. She slipped down between his legs and stroked him, tightening her grip.

"You've made me come," she said. "You need some relief, too."

Lowering her mouth over the tip, she pressed her tongue against it. She tasted herself and his pre-cum at the same time. She moaned at the appetizing flavor.

Holding her head, he urged her. "Fi, I'm close." Ned made the proclamation sound like a warning, as though he wanted her to stop.

But she didn't stop. As a matter of fact, his words spurred her on as she slid her mouth up and down him faster and faster.

Ned's legs tensed. Fiona eagerly accepted the cum that erupted from him. She swallowed and continued sucking him, lessening the intensity and pressure until they both collapsed into a pile.

Fiona crawled onto Ned's body, turned her head to the side and pressed her ear against his chest while her arm draped over him and her leg intertwined with his. Fiona's mind and body raced with emotions. Happiness, satisfaction, confusion, regret, fear. Fear being the nagging one, the one that kept saying, "I told you so."

After releasing a long, haggard breath, Fiona said, "Lesson Two. Compromise is a good thing."

# *Chapter 6*

## *Get to know your coworkers*

The constant and irritating beeping that Ned thought he'd imagined in his sleep didn't go away once he opened his eyes. Trying to adjust his gaze, he stared at his alarm clock that still flashed because of the power outage. Oh, so the annoying noise came from his watch. That's right. He had set it after the lights had gone off.

After pushing a side button on his digital watch until the noise stopped, Ned flopped his head back on his pillows to give himself some adjusting time before starting his day.

He swung his arm over to his side to wake his friend. Fiona had always slept in the same bed with him when there was a thunderstorm. This time wouldn't be any different.

"Get up, sleepyhead." His hand landed on a pile of pillows, but no Fiona. Sitting up, he surveyed his rumpled blue bed linens as though she couldn't be anywhere else but beside him. When he didn't see her in his room, he rubbed his eyes.

Where the hell could she be? Fiona was definitely not a morning person. She wouldn't have gotten up earlier than him and gone back into her own bed. Could she?

Damn, this must have bothered her more than he thought.

Ned tossed his comforter off his bed and planted his feet on the floor. Once the cool, air-conditioned air hit his skin, he shivered. He'd almost forgotten that he hadn't put his pajamas back on after their marathon foreplay session last night. And if it hadn't been for the fact that they'd promised each other not to go any further than just heavy petting, he would have driven his hard cock right inside of her and shown her what friends were for.

He stood and headed for the door until he heard the shower start ... the shower in his bathroom. Like a compass, his feet directed him to the sound. He hadn't noticed his bathroom door had been closed until the shower started. He never closed the door.

Pushing it open, he peered inside, craning his head through the crack until he was able to enter. Once inside, he saw Fiona's lush body through his transparent shower curtain.

He rubbed his eyes again to make sure he wasn't dreaming. Was his sexy roommate, his best friend, the woman who had made him want to call in sick for work so that they could keep touching each other, licking each other, loving each other-- without the sex of course--standing in his shower, rubbing herself all over?

Fiona dipped her head into the streaming water then turned her gaze to him. His stomach twitched, wondering how she would react. Would she scream and demand he leave his bathroom at once? But then again, it *was* his bathroom she was using. She could have always used her own and hadn't. Would she carry on a conversation like nothing had happened last night? Or would she want to finish what they'd started? Ned's dick twitched up as he watched her and she stared back at him.

"Morning," she said casually.

Ned waved. A stupid move, but he wasn't sure of his voice yet.

"I got the coffee going in case you wanted some before you got in the shower."

He nodded.

"Or if you just want to shower now..."

It was all the invitation he needed. Pulling back the curtain, he smiled like a boy looking up a girl's dress for the first time. Through the steam, he caught a vision of perfection standing in his shower. With her back to him, Ned studied her body.

When he first met Fiona, she had long, wavy black hair. He'd loved it. He imagined running his fingers through it. Sometimes during classes, he'd sit behind her and touch the ends. That was until the quarterback of the football team caught him and made fun of him in front of the class.

Ned had thought Fiona would have called him a freak or something and turned him in to the teacher or principal. Instead she told off the quarterback and admitted that she liked having Ned play with her hair. Whether she really knew he was doing it or not, he never felt embarrassed showing his affection to her in public again.

He wrapped his arms around her while standing behind her, his hard-on pressing in the crack of her ass. She ground her behind closer to him, purposely smoothing his cock between her cheeks. He groaned.

"Good morning to you, too," she said. She held up a bar of soap. "Get my back?"

He kissed down her neck to her shoulder before taking the flowery scented soap. She must have brought it from her bathroom. He only used soap that Fiona called a 'non-fragrant block of wood.' Hell, he was a guy. What did he care about smelling like a rainforest or an April shower? Now on her, all of that sweet-smelling stuff worked.

He lathered up his hands and set the bar in its dish. "What are you doing up so early?" he asked as his hands started rubbing at the back of her neck and made their way down her smooth, curvy back. He couldn't wait to get to her plump ass. He would set up camp there and never leave.

"Too wound up to sleep." Her voice echoed off the walls. "What about you? Sleep well?"

"Mmm, very. We should have done this instead of drinking warm milk and eating oatmeal raisin cookies."

She laughed until his hands got to her ass. Palming a cheek in each hand, he massaged them, letting the soap and water make his hands slick against her skin.

"Coffee, early morning shower. How does a man get this lucky?" he asked.

She turned around. Although she was five-foot-nine, Ned still towered over her. Hooking her hands behind his head, she brought him down to her.

Hesitating, he said, "I have morning breath."

Ignoring his warning, she kissed him anyway, sliding her minty-fresh tongue into his mouth. His head felt light, as light as the rising steam in the shower.

When she pulled back, she smiled and said, "Yeah, you do have morning breath."

He smiled. "I told you."

"Good thing I like you."

"You just like me?" His fingers trailed down her body and stopped at her dark nipple. He rolled the nipple around his thumb and listened as her breathing increased to a heavy pant. Taking her hand, he brought it down to his throbbing cock.

Not to be outdone, Fiona took his hand that was on her breast and slid it between her legs. "You never answered me," he began. "Why are you up so early and in my shower?"

With her soapy hand, she stroked him, coaxing him to give her the same treatment. "I wanted you to be in a good mood."

"Oh, I am in a good mood. A great mood." He pressed her back against the wall and with just the motion of his hand, got her to open her legs, bracing one on the side of the tub as his fingers smoothed against her nether lips. With each pass up, the tip of his finger brushed against her swollen clit.

She closed her eyes, still massaging his cock.

He lowered his mouth to her ear. "So tell me why you want me in a good mood."

"If I don't?"

He slid his middle finger inside of her while his thumb rested on her clitoris. She squeezed her eyes shut and had to momentarily stop milking his cock. She looked gorgeous. But even beautiful people had to be knocked down a peg or two.

"Oh! Ohh! Damn, baby! What are you doing to me?" she asked.

"I have vays of making you talk," he said in his best Colonel Klink imitation from *Hogan's Heroes*. It was awful, but it always made her laugh.

"Oh yeah? Then I suggest you torture me."

"Okay." In one swift move he pulled his finger from inside of her. *That* was torture.

"No!"

He laughed and kissed her cheek. "You're so easy." He slid his finger back inside of her.

Thinking of her sliding the tip of his dick inside of her boggled his mind. He wanted so much to plunge inside of her, feel with his penis what his lucky fingers had experienced.

But last night when the lights had come on and he'd seen the confusion in her eyes, he couldn't go on. As it was, he was slowly falling in love with her. He'd already loved her from just being her friend. But now he imagined a life with her ... and fully consummated sex.

"*I'm* easy? You're the one kissing me back while you slept. Every time I kissed your lips, you would kiss me back and smile."

He moved his finger in and out of her. "So that wasn't a dream."

"No, and neither is this."

As she stroked him faster, he, too, increased his speed. When he slid a second finger into her, she had to wrap her free arm around his neck to brace herself. Ned's legs shook and his breathing came out labored.

"Oh God, baby!" Ned leaned his head back, closed his eyes while a gush of warm sperm shot from his dick and landed on her hand and arm.

"Now your turn," he said and continued fingering her pussy. With his lips by her ear, he growled, "All I kept thinking about was coming inside of you. I want to feel how tight you are around me. I want your pussy to milk me dry. Tell me what you want, and I'll do it."

"Oh, Ned!" Her hand gripped his wet hair.

"Fuck it. I'm calling in sick today. We'll spend all day at home."

She shook her head. "No. You can't."

His thumb caressed her clit. Call in sick? Hell, he would quit his job if he could love her full time.

"Why can't I?"

In one breath she blurted, "Because I called your job and made plans to have dinner with your boss tonight." Then she came.

* ~ *

Fiona hadn't expected Ned to go so quiet. But after her explosive orgasm and her equally explosive confession, he'd done just that. As she sat on his bed wearing one of his T-shirts, she watched him get dressed.

"You're mad," she said.

"No." But he didn't look at her.

"Bullshit."

"Confused is more like it." Then he stared at her like she was a stranger.

"I don't understand your confusion. We agreed to this."

He raised his eyebrows. "We did? Was this something else you got me to do while I was sleeping?"

"Don't be an asshole. The whole plan behind us appearing as a couple was so that you can get ahead in your job and I can get that letter of recommendation or meet Kristoff. That's still what we want, right?"

He straightened his tie but continued staring at her until whatever argument he'd been running through his head had been resolved.

"Yeah. Fine." He picked up his jacket. "I just thought that we would both be planning events like this together so that there are no surprises."

She followed him when he stomped out of the room. Mean Ned may not be fun, but damn, this version of him was sexy too.

"Here. I got you something." She handed him a framed photo of herself.

Ned stared at it in her hand first before finally accepting it. It was a picture he'd taken on their trip to Cancun during spring break their last year of college. A long-haired Fiona in a sundress sat on a pier, feet dangling in the water. The shot itself wasn't extremely sexy, but Fiona, as usual, looked beautiful. Hot enough for his purposes, but not too revealing.

"What's this for?" he asked.

"Your desk. If we're supposed to look like a couple, you need to have at least one picture up of me. Makes this all look believable."

Ned rolled his eyes and shoved the frame into his briefcase. "You want to put some lipstick on and kiss me on the cheek so that it leaves an imprint? Or how about I unzip my fly and pull out my shirttail so it looks like had sex before work? I don't like all of this plotting and scheming. I would like a promotion based on merit, not on the idea that I may or may not have a hot girlfriend."

She got in front of him before he reached the kitchen to get his coffee. "Okay, you're right. I'm a bitch and you're right. I should have talked to you first before setting up the dinner. I had no right to do that." She tilted her face down and batted her eyelashes. She'd gotten his Nas 'Illmatic' CD, the last slice of pizza every time they ordered one and the remote control by giving him that look.

"Oh, no. You're not getting out of this with 'The Look.'" He filled his travel mug with coffee. But before leaving, he stood in front of her, his gaze bearing down on hers. "And you're not a bitch. Don't ever call yourself that and don't ever think that about yourself." He kissed her forehead. "Love you like a rock."

She waited until the door closed behind him before she said, "I love you, too, Ned Cholurski."

* ~ *

Even though the idea of having dinner with his boss supremely pissed him off, Ned couldn't be mad at Fiona. Even if he'd forgotten their plan, she hadn't. She was willing to play

65

this out to the hilt. He had to give her credit for that. So the stint in the shower, was that because she wanted to or to get him to go for this plan?

He shook his head and continued on to his desk, ignoring the stares and whispers this time.

At his workstation, Ned opened his briefcase and pulled out the picture. He stared at it for a moment. He remembered the exact moment he'd taken the picture.

While all the other college students were running around nearly naked and fucking all over the place, Fiona kept her attention on him. They did everything together. And when she'd taken off her shoes and sat down on the pier to cool off her feet in the water, he couldn't help but snap the shot. She looked absolutely--

"Beautiful."

A voice broke Ned's concentration. He turned to see Nose-Picker standing next to him, eyeing Fiona like she was some twenty-foot tuna Ned had caught. He set the picture on his desk and faced his coworker.

"So that's the mystery woman, huh?" Nose-Picker pressed.

Ned remained tight-lipped as he sat down.

"Or did that picture come with the frame?" Nose-Picker laughed as he headed back to his desk. Asshole. Even with jerks like that in the world, Ned still didn't want to parade Fiona around like a prized pig. She was his friend. End of story.

He reached for the photo to turn it down when he felt a hand on his shoulder. Swiveling around, he found himself confronted with Fat Bastard's bulging belly.

"N-n-neil, right?"

Sad part about it was that Ned actually got excited thinking Bastard was about to get his name right for a change. His shoulders slumped down. "Ned. You're getting close. Got the first two letters right this time."

This time his sarcasm did make its mark. Fat Bastard's face twisted into a horrible expression and he cleared his throat.

"I had an interesting call this morning from your fiancée."

Ned's eyebrows shot up faster than he could control them. Fiancée? What was Fiona thinking? That wasn't a part of the plan.

"Really?" Ned asked.

"A dinner invitation. Although I don't make it a habit of dining with my employees in a social setting, I, uh..." His gaze turned to the framed picture of Fiona that Ned was going to cover and put away. "Oh, is that her?"

Ned looked at the picture, then at his boss. "Uh, yes. Yes, sir. That's her."

"Fiona, huh?"

Oh, *her* name he could remember. Ned had been working for this pig for almost three years and he still couldn't get his name right. Thank God for his secretary. If it wasn't for her all of Ned's evaluations would have been to Nate, Nick or Neil Cholurski.

"Looks like a lovely young lady."

"She is, sir." Ned smiled. That was his Fi.

"Tell you what." Fat Bastard reached into his jacket pocket and pulled out a business card. "You two meet me at this restaurant at seven tonight. I own a part of this place so dinner can be written off. We'll discuss your future, young man. I see wonderful things happening. Big, beautiful, wonderful things happening." His eyes never left the picture, especially when he described Ned's ascending career as big and beautiful.

That's when Ned slammed the picture down on its face. "Can't wait to see you tonight, then."

Fat Bastard rubbed his hand over his head and waddled away. Ned felt like he was setting his best friend up for slaughter. He couldn't do that to her--or to anyone, for that matter. He would go home, tell her what happened and they could respectfully cancel the dinner plans.

# *Chapter 7*

## *Learn to roll with the punches*

Sure, calling Mr. Chunti was a ballsy move, Fiona thought as she smoothed vanilla lotion over her arms. Sure, she knew Ned probably wouldn't have appreciated it. His silence and blank expression screamed his true feelings. Nice Ned was not happy.

She slathered the thick cream over her thighs until she could no longer see it but its aroma lingered. And sure, she knew that if this dinner didn't work out, they could throw the Fourth of July picnic out the window, along with Ned's promotion and her letter.

As much as she wanted to sabotage her own chances, she wouldn't want to take Ned down. He deserved a promotion and more. Each day that she thought about working in law, Fiona's chest tightened. Could she claim medical leave from a job she didn't have?

Fiona took a deep breath as she sat naked in front of her vanity. She'd done everything she could that day to get Ned's body and his incredible skills off her mind. She'd taken a walk through the nearby park, played with someone's dog and even tried writing poetry, something she hadn't done since high school. Unless she thought about Ned, she had no inspiration.

So she did the ultimate buzzkill. She'd called Judge Kristoff's office again. Although they'd said they would call her if they heard anything, she knew persistence would pay off. If not, they would surely remember her name.

Instead, she'd gotten a resounding, "We'll let you know." The *thunk* of the phone hanging up still echoed in her ears. How could people be this cruel? This was her life, not some flash in the pan. She wasn't asking for a pound of flesh. She wanted and needed a job. And she only wanted the best. Unfortunately, Judge Kristoff's criminal court in Virginia Beach was the best.

Fiona didn't want to end up as one of those ambulance-chasing attorneys. Doing that would confirm her former classmates assumptions that she couldn't be taken seriously. No, she couldn't settle.

She closed her eyes and took a deep breath. This plan had to work. If not, then what would she have? Nothing. No job. No career. Well, not the career people had in mind for her.

She'd gone so far with her desire to work in the law. The last thing she wanted to do was prove her former classmates, her parents and even Ned that she was indeed the flighty cheerleader from high school.

That perception was entirely her fault. Being head cheerleader allowed her to duck out of many of her classes to set up special events or run the pep rallies. Her disappearing acts from her classes coupled with taking some relatively easy courses, got her the nickname Lightning because she moved around quick, was exciting to look at but no one gave a second thought about her when it was all said and done. The nickname was ironic considering that lightning scared her.

But if she showed some effort, put herself out there like she really tried, then she couldn't be faulted. People would realize she'd been serious and the fates had dealt her a cruel blow. She could harm her chances and pump Ned up in the process. He truly should be doing more than just being Chunti's programmer.

If her new secret plan worked, this time she would move back home and Ned couldn't stop her. As much as she loved him and loved living with him, she couldn't continue leeching. He deserved better. Until now, though, she'd thought she would be it.

When she heard the front door slam, Fiona slipped on her white terrycloth bathrobe and went into the living room. Poor Ned looked dog-tired. She hadn't seen his head hang down like that since high school. His eyes carried more bags than a luggage cart at the airport. Must have been a really taxing day.

"Hey, hot potato," she began, trying hard to kick up his spirits. "What's shakin', bacon? What do you know, Joe? Come on. I have way too many of these and I can keep going."

She got a half smile for her efforts. Yep, a crap day.

Ned dropped his briefcase to the floor with a thud then plopped on the couch, face up. His arm immediately covered his already closed eyes. One leg stretched out on the couch and his other foot planted on the floor.

Fiona sat on the empty space between his legs, then crawled on top of him, her chin in his chest and her legs around his one on the couch.

"Want to talk about it?" she asked.

He let out a long breath. Wintergreen Altoid laced his exhalation.

Uh oh. Not good. He only downed Altoid mints when he was pissed off or angry about something.

"The fat fuck still doesn't know my name," he finally said. "But guess what?" He removed his arm from his eyes revealing his wild blue gaze. "He knows your name. One phone call and the man was drooling over your picture and talking about you like you were Oprah fucking Winfrey."

She winced. She could only imagine what it must have been like for him to go to work, have his boss not know his name but to completely recall hers. She combed her fingers through his shaggy brown hair.

"I'm sorry, sweetie. You know I didn't mean for that to happen."

He curled up his lips, which meant that he understood it wasn't her fault but the situation was shitty anyway. He'd made the same look when he used to let her sit in on his weekly poker games and she racked up every time.

"I don't know why we're even going to this dinner tonight. He's not going to discuss my future. He wants to look down your top and look at your tits and maybe see if he can get you on the side." He stroked his hand through her hair.

Ordinarily she would have yelled at him for ruining her hair that she'd spent an hour working on. But the man had had a rough day. If he wanted to run his fingers through her hair, so be it. Besides, she liked him touching her. Electric sparks shot through her body from her scalp down her back and through her feet.

"Look, I could call Fat Bastard and tell him you came down with something and we can't make it."

She shook her head. "No."

"I'm telling you. If he even so much as looks at you the wrong way, I'm going to stomp his ass."

And there was Mean Ned again. Too bad Mean Ned turned her on as much as Nice Ned and Silly Ned and Considerate Ned.

"Trust me. This will work," she said with assurance. "I promise you by the time he leaves dinner, he'll know your name, your intentions and your favorite drink."

"So he'll be like my wife but with short, fat, hairy legs." His eyes flashed. "Speaking of which, why did you tell him we were engaged?"

Oops. Something else she'd forgotten to mention that morning. But when she'd told that lie to Chunti, part of her had wanted it to be true. She wanted to be Ned's fiancée. But the way he looked at her now, he seemed ready to strangle her and hide her body in the trunk of her car. She swallowed before answering.

"I thought that if he believed you were getting married, that would show you were stable and a family man. I know. It truly just slipped out to him. When he asked me who I was, I panicked. I should have told you."

"Yeah, you should have." He reached down between them into his pants pocket. "I barely had enough time to get this." He produced a small red ring box that he set between his face and hers.

She gasped at the sight and bolted up. "What's that?" Not exactly the throttling she thought she would be getting, but now he surprised her more than she must have surprised him this morning.

A smile hitched up. "Don't worry. I told my mom the deal. She's hoping that we stop pretending and get together already."

His mom thought they were a good match? Fiona knew she'd always liked the woman. Not exactly flower children or free-wheeling seventies sexaholics, Ned's parents were a good mix between the two. Nevertheless, his mom was always a great mom at just the right moments.

With a slow but steady hand, she reached for the box. She cleared her throat, holding it like she was holding the control switch to a bomb.

"Did you want me to get down on one knee and do this right?"

"Not funny, Neddy." She cracked the box open and nearly fell off the couch at the sight of the jewelry. It was beautiful, an antique white gold ring with a heart-shaped diamond set in the center, surrounded with white diamonds, rubies and sapphires.

Ned took the ring out of the box. "Great-great-great-grandfather had this ring made in the late 1700's in honor of the birth of this country, hence the red, white and blue jewels, and in honor of the woman he married."

Sliding the ring onto Fiona's left ring finger, she noticed how much Ned's hands shook as much as hers. That alone made her heart pound--the thought that he could actually be as nervous as she felt.

Once the ring was in place, and fitting perfectly, she gazed at her friend. "Are you sure about this? We could always say that we're engaged but haven't gotten the rings yet."

"Nope." He sat up and swung his leg over her head so he could stand up. "If we're doing this, we're doing it right. But I should warn you, this may work for me but it may backfire on you. What if this judge guy doesn't want some newlywed working in his courtroom because he's afraid she'll be wanting to pop out babies soon?"

Fiona smirked. "That's easy. Tell him the truth. I don't want to have children."

The smile dropped from Ned's face. "Oh." Without another word, he slipped back into his room. She, of course, followed him.

"You're getting weird on me again. What's up? You've always known since we were teenagers that I've never wanted children." She sat on his bed as he stripped.

Sucking her lower lip into her mouth, she chewed on it to calm her raging desire to see him naked again. Her gaze fixed on his chest and stomach.

"Yeah, but I thought, I don't know, maybe you'd change your mind. See the possibilities." He tossed his shirt into his hamper in the corner of his room.

"I've already seen the possibilities. A dad who didn't want to hang around to watch his kids grow up and a mother who regretted the day she had each child. I don't want to put any child through that. I don't want anyone else feeling like a burden."

Ned had to have known Fiona would have felt this way. Didn't he find it odd that she'd wanted to spend so much time at his house? Hadn't he wondered why she never invited him over to hers?

"If you had the right partner, someone who wanted to be with you, support you and wanted nothing more than to share his life with you, wouldn't that be different?"

The undeniable longing in his eyes cut Fiona deep in her heart. Ned had a hard need to be with Ms. Right and have the perfect children. Not that these kids would never do anything wrong or be straight-A students. They would be perfect because he and his wife would have made them and raised them together.

Coming from a complete home, one with a mother who still baked cookies and brought glasses of milk to guests when they came over, and a father who, despite his two left feet, loved to dance for company, Ned had known nothing but a good family life. He would make a perfect husband and an attentive father someday ... but for someone else.

A cold feeling draped her body and she shook in response. Ultimately, her fantasy to be Mrs. Cholurski would be that, only a fantasy. No matter how he felt about her, he wanted a family. He'd made that clear even when they were younger. But for now, she had him.

"We're talking 'what-ifs' when we should be discussing our game plan." She sprang from the bed, determined to get beyond this topic of conversation and onto something they could truly agree on.

"Yes, what is the game plan, oh Mistress of the Dark?" he intoned, finishing with a stately bow.

"Very funny." She playfully slapped his bare arm. Touching him sent shockwaves of tingles up her arm. She had to stop touching him or they would never make it out of the apartment. "This is what we're going to do. I'm going to sit and smile. If Chunti asks me anything about us, I want you to answer. If he asks me specific questions, I'll turn them around so that it highlights you and your goals. At some point, I will leave the table. If he talks about my ass or my tits, you'll stand up for your, ahem, property."

"Pig," he spat.

"I know. He'll see you're a man protective of yours and back down, but he'll respect you for it. That's when you let him know that you have ideas that will benefit the company but by no means do you tell him any specifics. That unscrupulous bastard will take your ideas and run with them. Then you will leave and let me be with him alone."

Ned shook his head. "I don't like that part. What if he makes a move on you?"

"Come on. In the middle of a restaurant?"

"Yeah, one in which he is a part owner and can get a nice quiet booth by himself?"

She raised her hand. "Trust me. I can take care of myself. Remember I used to be a head cheerleader and had to ride in the same bus as the football and basketball players."

"I still don't like this. Seems like we're going through an awful lot to get what's rightfully ours. You're too damn good for that clerk's job for Kristoff. And I know I can run a great programming department."

"Remember, sweetie. It's not what you know but who you know."

Ned glanced at his watch. "Right now what I know is that we're running late. I need to get a quick shower."

"All I need to do is throw on a dress."

"Just make sure you don't miss."

"He's playing here all week, folks."

* ~ *

Ned sat in the living room, his leg twitching and his fingers drumming on his knees. He'd flipped through the one *Martha Stewart Living* magazine on the coffee table. Fiona's magazine.

So much for "throwing something on." What the hell was taking her so long? It was already a quarter 'til seven. He'd told her over and over again that night they had to be at the restaurant *at* seven.

He hated being late for anything. His mother even told him that he was born early too. A month early.

Jumping to his feet, Ned paced. "Come on, Fi. We've got to go."

Finally her door opened.

"It's about time." His mouth dropped open when he saw her.

A vision in red. She wore a red mini dress with a plunging neckline, one so deep if she bent over the right way, one could see her navel ... and lower.

"Are you sure you have that on the right way?" he asked.

"Well, I could turn it around but I don't think the back is any better." She turned around and he noticed two things: the open back was deeper than the neckline, cutting right above her luscious ass, and Fiona had hair, long, flowing hair. Looking at her from the front, her hair was brushed down and parted to the side. But in the back she had curls.

Knowing that he must have been staring at the extension, she quickly supplied, "I think I should look a little different. The hair should do it. Do I look like a slut?"

"Just my slut," he joked.

She sauntered to him. Brushing her backside against his crotch, she purred, "Of course."

He couldn't let her get away with that. With an arm around her waist, he pulled her close and kissed the back of her neck and shoulder.

"No, no, no. We have to go. We're going to be late." She put up a lame attempt to get free of his grasp but all she managed to do was wriggle against his cock even more, causing it to wake up. It didn't help that she smelled like vanilla and musk oil, and tasted just as sweet.

He wanted her. Right there and then.

"Fuck Chunti," he said, his thoughts materializing into words.

"No, fuck me." She turned in his arms. "Later." After giving him a quick peck, she slipped out of his arms.

He groaned. "You can make a sane man go crazy."

"Really? So what will happen to you? You're already half crazy."

"Whoa. Was that a rim shot I heard? You should take that act on the road."

He put his hand at the small of her back. Her warm flesh sizzled against his palm. God, he couldn't wait to get her back to the apartment. Call it research. Call it preparation. Whatever it was, he had to have her.

"Don't do anything to get me riled up during dinner," she warned as he locked the apartment door.

"Why's that?"

"I'm not wearing any underwear. I don't want to soak through this dress."

Oh yes. It would definitely be a long night.

# *Chapter 8*

### *It's all about marketing*

In the same way Ned's breathing would stagger when his doctor would tell him to breathe normally at his regular checkups, he couldn't stop thinking about Fiona sans panties.

At the table, she crossed her legs. Both he and Fat Bastard Chunti noticed. How could he not? Fiona's legs seemed to go from her neck right down through the floor. Long, luscious buttery-brown, shapely stalks he wanted to nibble on, lick, and wrap around his body for several hours, days even.

He picked up his glass of bourbon. He hated bourbon but Chunti insisted. Bringing it to his lips, he took a whiff of the alcohol, allowed his stomach to settle then set the drink on the table. So much for having his boss know what he liked to drink.

Fiona took a sip of her drink. "Mmm, this is good, baby." She held up her glass to Ned. "Try it." She winked.

Flashing a sheepish grin to his boss, Ned accepted the glass and took a sip. Amaretto Sour. God, he loved this woman. It was his favorite drink and one she didn't necessarily care for. She must have ordered it when Chunti made him get the bourbon.

"Good, huh?" she asked with a grin as big as the Starship Enterprise.

"Very." His voice lowered to an intimate level.

Why did Chunti have to be at the table? Licking his tongue over his lips, he wanted nothing more than to taste the Amaretto and her pussy juice right now. What a mix. He could just slip under the table and--

"So how long have you two been together, Fiona?" Mr. Chunti asked, swirling his whiskey around in his glass.

Forgetting their deal, Ned answered immediately, receiving a swift kick under the table in response. "Oh, we've known each other for it seems like forever." He got another kick for that statement. "But I would want to know her for the rest of my life and ten lifetimes after."

A hand on his thigh rewarded him for his honesty. Big mistake. Blood flooded the lower half of his anatomy until his dick twitched, his hand flicked and his knees bounced.

"We became best friends first." Ned retrieved her hand from his thigh and held it above the table. "Then we realized we were in love during our first year of college." He gazed at her, realizing he was opening a real part of his heart. "We were studying one night, late. In the library. They closed so we had to go to my dorm room. She had a roommate who was the floor snitch and my roommate didn't care who walked in the door as long as no one touched his beer."

That got a chuckle from Chunti.

Ned continued. "We sat on my bed. Little flashlight to study by. You remember that?"

Fiona smiled and nodded. Her gaze held a faraway look like she was remembering that time in her head and heart as well.

"I remember Fi fell asleep first. Right here." He swept his hand over his chest and down one arm. "She felt so light on me. I brushed her hair back. It was longer, um," he stopped, realizing that tonight she did, technically, have long hair, though it wasn't necessarily her own. "Longer than this then. And I held her the entire night. When she woke up, she kissed me. You thought I was asleep," he finished, turning to Fiona. "I wasn't."

Tears pooled in her eyes.

"Since then we haven't been apart."

She stroked her fingers down the side of his face. Curving her fingers behind his head, she brought him forward and gave him a sweet kiss that eventually turned into something more passionate. After her moan but before any tongues could be exchanged, she pulled back.

"Gentlemen," she said with a cracking voice, "I must excuse myself."

Ned stood when she did. Chunti, realizing how much of a jerk he looked by remaining seated when Fiona stood, lumbered up from his chair at the moment she walked by him and down the restaurant, every man's eyes on her to the disgust of every woman in the place.

She was stunning. A beauty with brains. Too bad she didn't want what he wanted, otherwise she would have been a great partner, a wonderful wife. Would have made his parents happy too.

But what was he thinking? That was exactly the problem. She was a beauty with brains. She was even a former cheerleader, for God's sake. He was sure she'd gotten her hand slapped from some sort of underground cheerleading council for befriending the school nerd this long. She probably got some sort of demotion for even thinking up and going through this crazy plan. But marriage? He knew she wouldn't go that far.

Despite their friendship, he was still Ned the Nerd and she would always be the beautiful girl who looked too good to be with him.

"I think she'll be safe going to the bathroom," Chunti said, breaking into Ned's thoughts. "It's okay for you to sit down now."

Ned hadn't noticed he was still standing until Chunti made mention of it. He took his seat but couldn't wait for Fiona to return.

"That's a nice girl you have," Fat Bastard said.

"She's an extraordinary woman." Ned was sure to stress the word 'woman.'

There was nothing girly about Fiona. Not her attitude. Not the way she dressed. Not even her scent. She was all woman. And if he wanted to get through dinner, he would have to stop thinking about her so that his cock could settle down.

"Every time I try talking about her, she talks about you. She must really love you, Nester."

An hour with this blowhard at dinner and he *still* couldn't remember his name.

"It's Ned."

Chunti lifted his drink. "Sorry. It's the booze talking."

Yeah, 'cause you never forget my name at work, asshole. Or maybe you're drunk every day you come to work. Maybe that's it.

Ned gave him a polite smile. "She's supportive of me. She sees me doing great things."

"Really? Like what?"

Don't share any of your ideas with him until you have the title. Fiona's words bounced around in his head. She was right.

"You know. Things I work on at home. But I think it would really put Meta on the map as far as software is concerned."

Without thinking, Ned picked up Fiona's Amaretto and gulped it down. He caught Chunti's bewildered expression. The bastard's eyes cut from the empty glass in Ned's hand to the full glass of bourbon on the table. Shit. He'd fucked up. Where was Fiona when he needed her?

"Oh no. Fiona's going to kill me," Ned covered, setting the glass down.

Chunti shook his head. "No big deal. We'll order her another one before she gets back." He snapped his fat fingers.

In the darkened restaurant, with its dark cherry wood tables and chairs, and black leather seat cushions in the booths, the Italian eatery could be either sinister or romantic. Ned surmised that the dinner companion dictated the mood. If he were here alone with Fiona, this place would be perfectly romantic. But as he sat at the small table with Chunti, he couldn't help but feel like he was making a deal with the devil.

The waiter whisked the glass away.

"Tell me the truth, son."

Hearing Chunti call him son made Ned bristle. He quivered and had to blame the air conditioning for his sudden chill. Chunti seemed to buy it.

"Where do you see yourself five years down the road?"

This was Ned's big chance. He could talk about himself, his potential, to his boss. If only Fiona was there to see it. "I see myself heading up the software programming department."

Chunti cocked a half-smile. "That's my job. You trying to tell me something?"

"Yes, you should be promoted to a higher position and I should have your job." He didn't know if it was the alcohol or the raging hard-on that slowed in going down, but he felt cocksure about himself.

"You're either a very intelligent man or the stupidest fuck in the world." He howled out a big, belly laugh.

"Considering you can't remember my name, I'd say I'm the smartest one here." Ned spoke a decibel below Chunti's laughter. Didn't mean the Fat Bastard didn't catch it.

"Look, I'm bad with names. I admit it. But I do recognize potential."

"And when did you recognize that potential, Mr. Chunti? When you heard about my fight or when you saw my fiancée?" Ned wasn't looking to make friends. If Fiona knew what he'd said, she would have kicked him hard enough to break his shin.

"Honestly? The fight. I figured you for a fruit but it's usually the gay guys that are better employees anyway."

This was wrong on *so* many levels. The man must be drunk, high *and* suicidal. Ned blinked at Chunti's candor.

"There's a few people I want you to meet at my house this weekend. But so that I'm introducing you to the right people, give me an idea of what you're doing."

Ned hesitated. His in-your-face attitude hadn't failed him yet. Maybe this would work too. Leaning forward, he shared a part of his idea that involved cell phones, e-mail and paging services, something not currently on the market.

He saw the flash in Chunti's eyes. Ned had hit on something, but purposefully he held back a lot of the specifics. If Chunti was a crook, and if he'd planned on stealing this idea, he would need to know the drawbacks. Chunti wouldn't get that information from Ned even if he offered him a Cuban cigar and a million dollars.

"Cigar?" Chunti asked and held up two of them.

Ned's mouth dropped open just as Fiona came back to the table.

"I see you gentlemen have been keeping busy," she said as the waiter set a new drink down for her. She glanced at Ned, who only shrugged his shoulders.

"Trying to convince your fiancé to join me for a hearty after dinner smoke. I don't think he's up for it."

"I am." She slid the tightly wound, leather-looking cigar through her index and middle fingers, shaped like a 'V.' Hesitating for a moment while she established eye contact with Chunti, she eased the cigar from his grip.

"Here." Chunti fished through his pants pocket. "Let me clip the end for you."

Fiona chomped the end off with her teeth and spat the tip onto the table. Not the most ladylike move in the world but damn, that was sexy!

"You can give me a light." Placing the long cigar between her full, red lips, she leaned close to Chunti and waited for him to light her tip. A surge of jealousy coursed through Ned's body as he watched her ooze sexiness to this cretin.

Ned threw a possessive arm around her. She responded, not by folding into his arms or putting her hand on his knee as she'd done before, but by spilling her drink in his lap. If his erection hadn't gone down before, he was certainly flaccid now.

"Oh no! Baby, I'm so sorry." She set her cigar in the ashtray and rubbed his lap with her cloth napkin. With a couple of the strokes, she got him. He could tell they were purposeful by the way she glanced at him and smiled.

"Did I get it all?" she asked.

"You got some of it." He took the napkin from her hand and dabbed the rest away.

"Maybe you can go in the men's room and clean yourself up a bit," Chunti butted in.

Fiona's eyes widened. "Yeah! Go put some cold water on it."

So that was her plan. She didn't have to pour a whole glass of alcohol on his lap to get him to leave the table. Eventually, after letting Chunti know she was his woman, he would have gone.

* ~ *

After excusing himself from the table, Fiona lifted her cigar in one hand and the glass of bourbon in the other. She took a quick gulp of the bourbon. Holding back the urge to cough when the alcohol burned her throat, she immediately took a drag from her cigar.

"Tell me the truth, Fiona," Chunti began. "What's this game you two are trying to run on me?"

If the alcohol didn't make her cough, then Chunti's accusation did. "What are you talking about?"

"This." He held his hands up. "You two. No way in the world can someone as hot as you want a guy like Ted."

"It's Ned."

"Whatever. You look like a..." he considered, licking his tongue over his lips, "...a smart gal..."

"I am." She leaned closer to him. "At least that's what my law professors all thought."

Chunti eased back. "Law professors?" he repeated.

"Didn't Ned tell you? I'm going to law school. I want to be a district attorney but I can't seem to get in to the right court to clerk for the best judge in Virginia Beach." She wanted to pout but thought the gesture would go over the top. It was enough to get this guy scared that she knew the law and could sue him eight ways to Sunday.

"Oh, good for you." He wiped his forehead. "Wish I could help."

Fiona took a deep breath, raising her chest up and out. "Yeah, me too." Then she took a slow, deliberate drag from her cigar and blew out smoke rings. Along with how to beat guys at poker, she'd learned the art of smoking a cigar and ways to make interesting shapes with the smoke. She still had the touch. But she could only push Chunti so far before he got suspicious. The idea of her meeting Kristoff had to be his idea.

"I love Ned," she began. "I would do anything for him. And he would do the same for me."

"That's beautiful." He put his hand on top of Fiona's.

A frisson of revulsion went up her arm and down her spine. She trembled slightly for effect. "Air conditioning."

Chunti nodded and asked a waiter to adjust the thermostat. "What made him want to fight someone the other night?"

"The guy put his hand on me inappropriately."

He immediately withdrew his and scanned the restaurant for Ned. "Just comforting you, dear. Nothing else."

"Of course." She took another puff. "I look forward to seeing you again at your party this weekend. I'm so excited."

"Good." Then Chunti's eyes got wide like headlights on a Hummer. "Hey, I have a close friend who's a criminal court judge. You may have heard of him. Kristoff."

Fiona allowed herself a considering look. "That name does sound familiar."

"I could introduce you to him at the party."

Bingo! And it came off as his idea. Men were so easy.

"Could you do that? I would really appreciate it." She put her hand to her chest knowing where his eyes would be directed. "It's no wonder Ned likes working for you."

"He's a fine employee," he said, his eyes still trained on her chest. "That's why I invited him to my annual picnic. He'll rub elbows will all the V.P.'s."

"How exciting. And just so you know, Mr. Chunti, I don't normally dress like this. Ned likes me to look this way when we go out."

Even though that was partially true, Fiona had to crank up the heat, show this guy that Ned was her number one priority and he thought the same of her.

After a hard swallow, he asked, "And what does he make you wear when you're at home?"

Fiona furrowed her eyebrows and tilted her head. "Wear at home? I don't wear anything at--oh, hey, baby." She rose from her seat and accepted Ned into her arms. She smiled to herself as Chunti choked on his bourbon, coughing uncontrollably.

"Sir, are you okay?" Ned pounded his boss on the back until whatever that was caught in his throat came up or went down.

"Fine. I'm fine." He took a sip of water then said, "You have a fine fiancée here. A fine one. And smart. If I were you, I would hold onto her."

Ned gazed down at Fiona. "I plan on it, sir."

# Chapter 9

## *Location, location, location*

*Come on! Come on! Send that big windbag on his way.*
Fiona had waited patiently through dinner. As she watched Ned
giving his boss a drawn-out good-bye, she couldn't wait to get
Ned home. And she hadn't really thought about jumping his
bones at all ... until he touched her back.

While they'd sipped their after dinner coffees, Ned lazily
placed his hand on the back of her neck. She remembered she'd
jumped, not used to the intimate touch from a man in public in
such a long time. But it had felt so good. So right. His thumb
had made easy sweeping motions over her shoulder while his
fingers circled her bare back.

Whatever Ned and his boss had been talking about hadn't
registered. At one point, she'd remembered closing her eyes.
When his hands trailed down her back, she straightened her
posture. It had felt like a feather dancing over her skin. Her
nipples had hardened against the silky fabric of her dress.

Damn, why did that Fat Bastard have them turn the a/c down? At that point she'd really needed it.

Now she needed to go home. "Nice meeting you, Mr. Chunti," she said, trying to cut their conversation short.

"You too, Fiona." He wrapped his chubby fingers around her hand.

Her stomach churned like it had when he'd touched her in the restaurant. Couldn't the man take a hint? He made her skin crawl every time he touched her. But instead she smiled and slipped her hand from his at an appropriate time.

"See you this weekend," Chunti said before going to his car.

Ned put his hand at the small of her back and led her to where he'd parked behind the restaurant. He snickered as though he'd thought up a joke he wasn't willing to share.

"What?" she asked, demanding that he share.

"That dress."

She could almost hear him follow with, "What were you thinking?"

But he said, "That dress" in a way that sounded like he was thankful that she wore it.

"I can get out of it in one move." She winked.

He growled. Had she known teasing Ned would be this easy she would have done it years ago.

"So what did you two talk about when I went to the bathroom?" Ned asked.

She smiled. A hint of jealousy tinged his question. "Why? Are you afraid that I might want to start a relationship with Chunti?"

"Very funny."

"No, I can see it. He would leave his wife because I could never be some man's mistress. And since he's older he wouldn't want any more children."

"Cut it out."

"Then he can keep a picture of me on his desk. But don't worry. You can always come by his office and masturbate to it."

"Yeah? Well, how do you think he would feel knowing that I licked your pussy?"

Hearing Ned talk dirty made her clit twitch. It throbbed in concert with her rapid heartbeat. She licked her tongue over her lips, intrigued with the idea of taunting him even more.

"It might turn him on." It was certainly turning *her* on just thinking about it.

He chuckled. "I'm sure he wants to hear all about the way you taste."

"And how's that?"

He caught her gaze as they continued to the car. "Sweet but bitter. Like honey and salt combined."

"He might think you're talking about honey-roasted peanuts." She tried lightening the sexual tension, but Ned's heavy breathing proved he wasn't in a joking mood.

"Maybe I need a refresher." Pulling her into a dark alley behind the restaurant, he pinned her against the wall next to a dumpster. Not the most romantic place in the world but it would do.

Semi-private. It was the semi part that got her juices flowing. At any moment someone could walk by and see them, huddled in the shadows, clawing at each other like animals, like teenagers, like lovers. Ignoring the smell and the way the jagged brick wall cut into her back, she stared into his eyes.

His lips crushed hers in a passionate kiss. Her body became pliant in his arms, bending to his will. Her hands held his arms to steady herself while one leg wrapped around his to draw him in closer. She felt his hard cock through his pants, pressing against her sex.

The humid summer weather did nothing to cool down her skin. A layer of sweat formed on her. She felt how hot his body became when she placed her hand at the back of his neck and touched the dampness in his hair.

His mouth traveled to her ear in a trail of kisses while his hand touched her bare chest and slid down to her breast.

"I can't believe you're completely nude under this dress," he mumbled in her ear. "No bra." His other hand gravitated to her thigh, then crept up under her dress confirming what she'd already told him before dinner. "Damn, no panties." He lifted his head to gain eye contact. "I thought you were saying that to get me going."

"Did it work?" she asked, nearly breathless.

"Hell, yes."

She laughed until the crash of the restaurant back door cut the mood. A busboy, coming out for a smoke while he dumped trash, nearly spat his cigarette from his mouth when he saw Ned and Fiona by the dumpster. Ned pulled his hand from her breast and pulled her around so that she could make the necessary adjustments to cover herself again.

"I know that cat is around her somewhere," Ned said, scanning the ground looking for that imaginary lost pussy. "Here, kitty kitty kitty."

Fiona, trying hard not to burst into hysterical laughter, joined him in looking for this cat further down the alley. "Here, Chewy."

"Chewy?" He continued down the alley, careful not to stop under a streetlight.

"If I had another cat, I want him to be a big, bushy one. Something that looks like Chewbacca from *Star Wars*."

"You're kidding, right?"

"I never joke about The Force."

Ned sighed. "Maybe we should head back to the car. Finish what we started there."

In this instant-gratification, microwave life, Fiona wasn't satisfied with waiting. Ducking into a darkened crevice, a four-foot space between two buildings, she brought her shoulders forward, letting the top of her dress fall down to her waist.

"If you're scared, say you're scared."

As though she released a madman, Ned pressed his body against her partially exposed one and kissed her hard, letting his tongue probe her mouth. He tasted like Amaretto and mint. His hands couldn't touch enough of her, grabbing and moving over every inch of her flesh. Both hands cupped her tits. She felt her nipples strain to a painful hardness as his palms brushed against them.

"Neddy, oh fuck!"

His mouth covered her nipple and it made her draw her breath in sharply. The only way she could hold herself up was by putting one hand to his shoulder and running her fingers through his hair. She tried locking her knees back but they, too, felt like jelly.

"Your body feels so good," he said between sucking and licking. His tongue twisted around her nipple until the pleasure was too much to take.

Her body trembled. She begged him not to stop. And he didn't. Capturing her nipple between his lips, he tugged on it, enough so that she screamed in ecstasy. He knew how to work her body.

His mouth performed the same magic on her other tit. Licking, laving, sucking until she, again, screamed, writhed in pleasure. If the neighbors weren't calling the cops yet, they would be soon, especially since Ned started kissing down her stomach. Then he raised her short dress to her waist so that she was completely exposed, her dress now a belt hanging loosely around her.

Without a word, he guided her leg to rest on his shoulder. While rubbing his hand up and down her lower lips, sending sparks of electricity through her body, he said, "I have been thinking about this, about you, all through dinner."

After parting her folds, his tongue teased the tip of her clitoris. He flicked back and forth over it as she moaned louder and louder with each pass until finally his mouth fully took her in. He sucked her hardened nub causing her to grab handfuls of his hair.

When he dove his finger inside of her pussy, Fiona slammed back against the wall. Mistake. A jagged piece of brick pierced her skin.

"Ouch!" she screamed.

Ned immediately stopped. No sucking. No finger. He gave her his full attention. "Did I hurt you?"

"Not you. The wall." She'd been cut right between her shoulder blades.

Standing, Ned pulled down her skirt. Pulling her into the light, he turned her back to him to examine the cut.

"Damn."

"Is it bad?" She couldn't see it but it stung like hell. Was that blood dripping down her back or sweat?

"It's not pretty. Let's get you home so I can clean this up." He attempted to get her dress back on her shoulders but she stopped him.

"Don't stop. I need you." Guiding his hand back between her legs, she cupped his hand over her wet mound. Gazing into his eyes, she asked, "Don't you want me?" This time pouting was necessary.

He smiled. When he kissed her, she tasted her juices on his lips and his tongue. Sweet and salty.

Beyond her will, she leaned back, allowing Ned to take over. Mistake number two. Her back hit the same jagged brick and caused her to jerk forward, butting her teeth against his.

"Ow! I'm not into pain with my pleasure." He rubbed his upper gums.

"Sorry. I hit that brick again." She wrapped her arms around his neck and kissed him sweetly.

With a boyish grin, he said, "There's always the car."

Shaking her head, she replied, "There's more than one way to skin a cat."

"Don't tell that to Chewy."

Her hands reach down and eased down his zipper. Trust filled his eyes as she undid his belt and pants. His pants dropped down to the ground. When she went for his jockeys, his look encouraged her to continue.

"I can't believe I'm doing this." He stroked his thumb over her cheek.

Grabbing his shaft, she gave him one, long, tight stroke. "Believe it."

He was so thick in her hand. Pulsating and throbbing like it was its own animal. She wanted it inside of her, flesh to flesh, burrowing into her and branding her skin as she'd often dreamed.

Fiona continued stroking him, squeezing the pre-cum up to the tip. She wanted so much to lick it off. But not yet.

"Now, baby?" she asked.

"So close," he murmured with his eyes closed.

"Wait." She let him go, which caused him to look at her with wide eyes.

"What are you..."

He didn't have to finish the question. As soon as she braced her hands against the wall, her legs spread apart, and her ass to him, he must have known what she wanted, what she needed.

"No. Let's just go home. I'll tend to your back."

"I *need* you." Her voice climbed an octave. "If you want me to beg, I will."

"Fi, I want you. Lord knows I've been fantasizing about it for weeks, months, hell, years. But..."

"But what?" She gazed down at his cock, which was falling down faster than a beehive hairdo in a strong wind.

"I've always wanted to look at your face." He smoothed his fingers over her cheek. "I want to see what you look like when I'm inside of you. I want to see you come."

Her juices flowed until she thought they would run down her leg at any moment. "You're torturing me." Grabbing his cock again and this time cupping his balls, she stroked him while massaging his tight balls. "We have all night. I'll get on top of you and ride you. Would you like that?"

He grunted.

"Or maybe you like it the old fashioned way, me on the bottom. Legs spread for you, pussy all nice and wet. Nipples all hard. You can pound into me as hard as you want, or do it nice and slow."

He groaned.

"Or maybe you want to watch me pleasure myself. I have a vibrator in my bedroom that's not as big as you but can still do the..."

He didn't allow her to finish. Removing her hands from his penis and balls then spinning her around, he put her hands back against the wall.

"God, you drive me crazy." Sliding the tip of his cock up and down her doused nether lips, Fiona braced for his entry.

Ned pushed the tip inside of her and held it. His thick tip spread her, sending goose bumps all over her body and making her shiver with excitement. How he managed to just hold his cock inside of her without moving amazed her. But she didn't have that type of self-control. She pushed back against him, trying to drive him inside of her but he held her waist to keep her in her position.

"I've waited twelve years for this," he growled. "I'm going to damn well enjoy it." With one thrust, he was inside of her to the hilt.

Fiona couldn't believe it. With that thrust, she had an instant orgasm. Explosions rocketed from her filled pussy up through her body and to her brain, pushing her into sensory overload. She screamed, digging her manicured fingernails into the wall and nearly falling to her knees. If Ned hadn't had his arm around her waist, she would have crumpled to the ground in a satisfied, quivering mess.

Ned pulled out all the way to the tip and slammed his thick cock inside of her again. And he did it again and again until his rhythm picked up and so did her beating heart.

His last girlfriend was an idiot.

He pressed his chest against her back, his head next to hers. "I can't hold out much longer, babe. Fuck, you're so hot and tight inside. It's better than I thought it would be."

Why the hell would he be sorry? He'd already given her a pretty amazing orgasm just from entering her. She had to give him the same in return. Plus there was always what could happen back home.

Reaching his hand down, he parted her labia lips and rubbed her swollen clit. Ecstasy started swirling again in her lower abdomen as her legs quivered. Leaning her head back, she let out another scream as she came again, harder than the first time.

"I can't hold out, babe," Ned said, almost like a warning.

Although she longed to have him come inside of her, she wanted to do something special.

"Pull out," she said in a hoarse whisper.

Without question, he did so. She turned in his arms, lowered herself to her knees in front of him, held his slippery shaft and eased him into her waiting mouth. The concoction of her juice and his pre-cum tasted wonderful. She couldn't wait for his sperm.

He held the back of her head. With slow and easy thrusts, he pumped his cock into her mouth as he'd done moments before in her pussy. True to his word, he was ready.

"Fuck!"

Warm cum squirted into her mouth and she swallowed, trying hard not to let any of his juices escape her mouth and fall on his clothing. It was bad enough she'd had to spill her drink on him just to get him to leave the table earlier.

Fiona licked the length of his cock and kissed the tip at the end of the journey. Ned helped her to her feet. With hands framing her face, he drew her in for a kiss.

When he pulled back, she rewarded him with a smile. "That was lesson four."

"And what's that?" he asked, grinning.

"You can make any location work for you."

# *Chapter 10*

## *Satisfy your customer*

Ned wrapped his legs around Fiona as they sat in the bathtub in her bathroom. He didn't know who designed the apartment. Ned had the biggest bedroom but Fiona's room had the bathroom with the biggest bathtub. That suited him fine. Fiona was more of a bath person anyway, whereas he was fine with a quick shower. Taking a bath together, however, changed his mind completely on the whole bath concept.

His mind still reeled from what they had done in the alley. Never had he been that wild or reckless. Anyone could have walked by them and seen them. They would have seen her round tits swinging back and forth as he pounded her pussy from behind. They would have seen her firm ass. And unfortunately they would have also seen his naked behind.

"No more low-back dresses for you for a while." He pressed a wet washcloth to her wound. When she flinched, he eased up on the pressure.

"Too bad. I was going to wear this cute little halter top at the barbeque on Saturday that just..."

"Oh no, you weren't. Turtlenecks and pants. Baggy pants. That's what you're going to wear."

"To a barbeque in July?" She laughed. "Don't worry. I'm keeping it very conservative."

Not exactly how he saw this night ending. He for sure didn't think he would actually have sex with her. But what a feeling. Tight, hot, wet, pulsating, passionate. All the things he knew it would be and more. Why the hell hadn't he told her a long time ago how he felt?

Oh, yeah, because he didn't want to ruin their friendship.

Cleaned up, the cut wasn't so bad. Mostly scratches. In the alley, though, it looked worse. It took no time for the blood that oozed from it to dry and crust on her honey-colored skin. And when he'd pressed his chest against her back, some of her blood had stained his shirt. A sad reminder of an unbelievable time. He bent forward in the tub and kissed the spot, making her moan.

"You think I'll have a scar?" she asked, sounding too concerned about a topical abrasion.

"Big one. Huge. I'm thinking of calling you Scabby from now on."

She twisted around and slapped his arm playfully. "You are not funny."

"And yet, again, you're laughing."

She laid her body on his chest and he held her. A warm bath, candles lit, a beautiful woman in his arms who was his best friend. It didn't get much better than this.

In the dimly lit bathroom, he never noticed how she had decorated it. Still all off-white including the bathtub, the walls, the sink and the countertop, she'd hung pictures of fruit all around, apples, bowls of grapes, cherries. Kind of odd for a bathroom. Maybe for a kitchen or even a living room. But that was his Fi. Always marching to a different beat.

A multicolored shag rug covered the floor by the tub. A purple flower in a decorated pot sat on top of the toilet tank. And she had a clear shower lining and a shower curtain covered with more fruit, watermelon, bananas, peaches, oranges. This woman had a serious obsession with food.

"If I tell you something, you promise not to get angry?" she asked.

"No. So tell me. What did you do this time, Lucy?" he asked, trying to make her laugh with his Ricky Ricardo accent.

"But, Ricky, I want to be in the show."

Thank God she got the joke.

"Seriously," she began, "your last girlfriend, Megan, she told me you were lousy in bed." Fiona's body tensed, obviously preparing for Ned to go crazy.

Instead he stroked his bubble-covered hand over her arm. "I was."

She blinked and brought her head up so she could look into his eyes. "*Excuse* me?"

"Oh, yeah. I was horrible. Wouldn't move. Could barely get it up. Would never go down on her. Fell asleep right afterward."

"You've *got* to be kidding. And you're proud of this?"

"Not really. But she wouldn't take the hint that I didn't want to have sex with her so she kept pushing." He soaped his hands and rubbed them down her arms and sides. "Obviously, I'm different with someone I want to be with."

She hummed, vibrating his body and awakening his dick once more. He could go another round with her. Right here. Right now.

Squirming like a fish, she flipped onto her stomach, then slid up his body to meet his face. What a feeling!

"We're still good, right? Still friends." She had a questioning look in her eyes that scared him.

"Yes, of course. Why would you ask?"

She let out a long breath. "Just wanted to be sure."

"I love you like a rock. Scars and all." He gave her a slap on her ass and a squeeze for good measure.

"Hey!"

He laughed but, looking at her, he suddenly became serious. "What's going to happen when we get what we want?" he asked. "Fat Bastard said he's going to introduce me to some important people at his party."

"And I'll get to meet Judge Kristoff. That was all Chunti's idea." She winked. "Just like you said. We'll be fine."

"But will we be a couple or..." His voice trailed off.

She jerked up to a kneeling position and let the bubbles slide down her voluptuous body. "I know this. I need my doctor."

Hearing that made Ned bolt straight up. "Your back?"

He'd thought the scratches were just that. Scratches that would heal in a few days. Maybe there had been a nail in the wall that had gone deep. She'd said she was fine. But damn, why hadn't he take her to the emergency room like he wanted instead of listening to her?

She stood up and stepped out of the tub. After nodding her head, she said, "Yep. It hurts really bad, Doc. What can you do to help me?"

His face relaxed as a smile eased up. He got it. He understood that she wanted to role play, and she didn't want to talk about them, a subject they couldn't ignore for very long. Doctor and patient? He could get into that game.

"So what's step one, Doc?" she asked, still dripping as she stood on the shaggy bath mat. "Shouldn't my wound be dry?"

He step out of the bathtub and drained it. Then after blowing out each candle, he said, "Step one is that you call me Doctor Cholurski."

Fiona raised her eyebrows, impressed to see Ned willing to play along. It was better than talking about their relationship when she hadn't figured that out yet. The same questions had rolled through her mind. What would they do after this charade was done? She loved him. They were great friends. He could definitely satisfy her sexually. But, for one thing, he wanted a relationship with someone who wanted a family. That wasn't her. And she couldn't bear to see him with another woman, starting his life with someone else. So for now, they would play.

"I'm sorry, Dr. Cholurski." She bowed her head demurely. She knew a dominant personality existed in him. She'd opened the door to it in the alley. Now she was ready to see him explode.

"You are right about one thing." He retrieved a white, fluffy bath sheet and swaddled her body. "You and your wound need to be dry." Then he leaned down to her ear. He growled, "But that's all that had better be dry."

She buckled. Like a superhero, he swooped her up into his arms and carried her into the bedroom.

"No, let's go to your room," she said.

He furrowed her eyebrows, questioning her choice. Her bed was right there, unmade but there.

She quickly explained, "You have a bigger bed."

He smiled. "You think this doctor needs a lot of room to work?"

She crossed her legs while in his arms. "No. But this patient might."

He took her to his bedroom. Once he set her on his bed, he continued drying her, then said, "You'll do exactly what I say."

She licked her tongue over her lips. "Yes, Doctor."

"Now before I get started, I need to dry off." He held out the towel to her.

After smacking her lips and cocking her head, she whined, "You mean I have to be your patient *and* your nurse? Why can't your nurse do that?"

Ned's eyes widened. "Oh, I can bring another woman in here?"

Snatching the towel, she glowered at him. "Now that you put it that way, I guess I can do my part."

"This is what happens when you have an HMO."

Fiona laughed as she patted the towel over his broad shoulders and down his toned arms. She swept the towel down his chest to his rock-hard abs. She was amazed that she hadn't noticed until recently what a fine physical specimen her erstwhile nerdy friend had become.

He was way different from the boy with stringy arms, no ass and pencil-thin legs. Now, although still no Adonis, he was certainly not out of shape. He had what she and her girlfriends used to call a swimmer's body. Long muscled arms, broad shoulders, a back wide at the top and tapered down to his waist, a nice firm ass, and legs that looked like he spent the majority of his time hiking, jogging and biking. When did he have time to work out?

She took notice of his room and realized how much it reflected Ned's personality: very organized. His bed sat perfectly centered in the middle of the room. A twenty-seven inch flat screen TV with a built in VCR and DVD players topped a chest-high dresser that stood at the foot of his bed, perfect for watching porno, she suspected. Except for his bed and bathroom, the colors were standard apartment colors: drab beige. But on his bed, a deep cobalt blue comforter covered the queen-size sleigh bed. Next to the door on the side of the bed, his computer desk with all of his computer equipment took residence. She took in a deep inhalation and captured his scent, that musky, boyish smell that now drove her wild.

When he turned around, she dried his back, making sure to rub his taut ass for good measure. Then she moved her hands to the front of him, pressing his back against her chest, sure he felt her hard nipples poking him. Dropping her hands lower, she held his thick cock up while her other hand dabbed his balls. She felt him hardening in her hand.

"I'm not sure how your nurse does this, so please forgive me if I do it wrong," she cooed.

He held her wrists and, with gentle force, moved them away from him so he could turn to gaze at her. "My nurse doesn't talk as much as you do."

Ned was really getting into this dominating role. God, what a turn on!

He continued. "She does what she's told and never complains." With a strong jerk, he snatched the towel from her hands and tossed it to the floor. The molten lava that bubbled between her legs erupted.

"But I'm your patient. Don't you know why I've come to see you?"

Leaning forward, he brought his lips millimeters away from hers. She felt his hot breath on her mouth as she closed her eyes in expectation of a passionate kiss.

Then she felt his breath on her cheek. He was moving away but still she would not open her eyes. She didn't want to know what he would do to her, just experience it. When she felt his lip brush the shell of her ear, she shuddered.

"Tell me where it hurts," he whispered.

She swallowed. "Oh God, everywhere."

Ned laughed. She opened her eyes and glared at him.

"Sorry," he apologized, turning back into Nice Ned for a moment. "I never thought I would have you this eager."

"And you won't if you keep laughing." She attempted to jump off his bed but with a strong grip on her wrist, he stopped her.

"I apologize for my unprofessional behavior. It won't happen again." He eased her into a sitting position on the bed, her feet dangling over the edge. "Again, tell me where it hurts."

She let out a long breath. "My back."

With the precision of a bobcat stalking its prey, Ned circled the bed and climbed on and crawled behind her. "Ah, I see. And how did this happen?"

In a delicate manner, part doctor and part compassionate lover, he stroked his fingertips over the cuts. Her body tingled from his touch, causing her to sit up straighter and her pulse to quicken.

"I--I don't know if I should tell you, Dr. Cholurski. It's very embarrassing." Well, not to Fiona it wasn't. But for demure, dainty Fiona, this would be mortifying to say in front of anyone including her family doctor.

Ned leapt from the bed and ducked into his bathroom. When he returned, he held a tube of Neosporin. He was really taking this doctor thing seriously.

He took his position on the bed behind Fiona again and pressed his lips against her back, which made her gasp.

"I've seen and heard it all. Nothing will shock me," he said. "Tell me. Be very detailed." With delicate care, he smoothed the creamy ointment on her scrapes. Even that felt good.

She closed her eyes and tilted her head back as his other hand roamed her body. His hand traveled down to her soaking pussy.

"I met a man in a restaurant," she began. "He looked nice."

"Probably harmless." His finger found its way through her folds to rub her clit.

That made her body stiffen. She grabbed handfuls of comforter, hoping her heart wouldn't pound through her chest.

"I did think that." She couldn't catch her breath so the statement came out like a pant. "Thought he was a librarian or accountant."

"Was he?" Ned rubbed his fingers against his comforter, probably to remove the medicinal cream, then his hand crossed in front of her body to her tit. He massaged it.

"No," she answered through gritted teeth. "He said he was a master and he was looking for a sexual slave."

Fiona felt Ned's cock twitching behind her. She moved back to feel him pressed between her ass cheeks. That's when he sat behind her, sliding his legs next to hers and positioning his head on her shoulder. Pretty soon their breathing patterns matched. Only heat separated their bodies.

"And you went with him?" he asked.

She nodded. "I knew he wouldn't hurt me."

"But he did. Your back."

"Emotionally."

His fingers sliced between her pussy lips. "Talking about it now makes you wet. Did you like what he did to you?"

She nodded, unable to find the words to speak.

"Tell me what he did. Say it." His finger dove inside of her.

She reached her hand back behind her to grab his hair. Her hips tilted forward and she spread her legs, hanging them over his legs, to give him better access. But as giving as she was, he showed no mercy, pounding her pussy until all she heard was the sound of his finger sloshing in her juices.

"He fucked me!" she screamed. "He ripped my blouse off of me. That's how I got the scratches. Then he--then he--Oh fuck, Ned!" Her hips rose from the bed as she pushed his hand so that his finger could probe deeper.

He obliged her request by sliding in a second finger. Her heart thrummed and she thought she would crawl out of her skin if he didn't let her come soon.

As though he'd read her mind, in a sinister way, he removed his fingers from inside of her. Fiona was sure her screams could be heard for miles around as she turned to him and tackled him on the bed.

"Don't fucking stop! Why did you stop?" She attempted to grab his hand but he kept them over his head and away from her. No matter. She would go for what she really wanted anyway. Grabbing his shaft, she positioned herself over his cock, ready to plunge down.

He held her shoulders and pulled her down to the bed. "You didn't finish telling me what happened."

"Ned, if you don't let me come, I'll..."

He wagged his finger at her. "No, no, no. Now you're being hostile. I can't have that in my office." He jumped from the bed, taking the Neosporin. As though he knew she would come after him, he turned before she could move and said, "Stay right here."

After setting the tube on his dresser, he darted from the room. She heard the hall closet opening and closing, then his footfalls back to the room. In his hand he had two multicolored scarves. Gaudy scarves his mother knitted for him but Ned refused to let them go.

"On your back, head on the pillows," he demanded.

Fiona wanted to argue but she complied. He tied one wrist to one post. When he did the other, he gazed at her.

"As you can see, they aren't tight. You can get out of them at any time. If this freaks you out, tell me, okay?"

She nodded. Then he crawled back onto the bed.

"You're not going to do my legs?" As much as she liked to be in control, she was really getting into Ned taking over. And he was doing a fine job of making her body his. "I would have thought you would want my legs spread open so you can do a full exam. See everything I have."

Ned hovered over her body. "I want your legs wrapped around me."

So did she, but he eased her back down to the bed.

"Not yet," he said. Lying next to her, his hand covered her tit. "Open your mouth, please." He must have thought of how polite that sounded and repeated himself. "I mean, open your mouth." His tone held a much harsher demand than before.

Without smiling, she did so. He touched the tip of his finger to the end of her tongue. As he held it there, she closed her mouth and sucked on it.

After sliding his finger out, he replied, "Temperature seems normal."

The giggle she'd suppressed earlier came out now.

"You laugh now. Just wait until I do your Pap exam."

Before she could ask what that entailed, his mouth clamped on her tit. His newly moistened finger circled her other exposed nipple. Her body undulated, rippling with pleasure. Gripping the scarves, she pulled her arms down, wanting so much to hold him, run her fingers though his thick hair, caress his face.

Covering her tit with his large hand, he massaged it. "I can't feel any lumps." He winked. "As a matter of fact, I think these are the most perfect breasts I've ever seen. And as a doctor, I've seen them all." His lips made trails of hot kisses down her stomach. "Small ones." Another kiss. "Big ones." A lick and a nibble. "But none that have hard, dark nipples like yours. None that fit perfectly in my hands like yours."

"Damn it, Ned, if you don't fuck me now, I'm going to scream holy hell." Fiona wrapped her legs around his body as she stared down at him.

Confidence oozed from him as he crawled back over her body. "I was going to give you the oral exam." He licked his lips, making the churning in her belly crank up more. "But seeing how you're so pressed for time, I'll oblige you."

Fiona exhaled in relief as she spread her legs open for him. She would have to remember to play this little game with Ned again. He could be a really good bastard when he wanted.

While rubbing the thick helmet of his penis up and down her wet pussy lips, he said, "But there is one condition."

"What's that?" she asked then bit her lower lip.

"You can't come until I say so." With that he slammed into her to the hilt.

Just like in the alley, the onslaught of an explosive vaginal orgasm hit her hard. She wrapped her legs around him to tamp down the urge to scream out his name and bless his mother in one breath. The tension in her arms and the way she held him between her legs must have been a dead giveaway.

"Are you coming?" he asked in almost a demanding tone.

Unable to speak, she shook her head.

"I can feel your pussy clamping down around me. Oh, Fi. Stop or I'll have to pull out."

She knew he wouldn't. If the sex felt so great for her, it had to be good for him too.

"Don't stop. Please. I'm so close." Fiona tried to look into Ned's eyes but the feeling was too strong. She flopped her head to the side and squeezed her eyes shut.

"What did I tell you?" he asked, but not slowing his thrusts. "I'll stop. I want to control your pleasure. I want to tell you when to come."

With one strong tug, she managed to release one hand from the scarf. Her hand pressed against Ned's hip in an attempt to stop him. "If you keep going, I'm going to come. No ifs, ands or buts about it."

Ned hooked one leg around his arm and increased his pounding, almost like he was daring her to come.

"Don't ... come." The words came out staggered like his breathing. "Your pussy's so tight."

She managed to get her other arm free but instead of pushing him away like before, she pulled him in. She grabbed his ass cheeks, squeezed them and held him down to keep him inside of her.

It was apparent that the master was buckling to his baser needs. He wanted to come. If she could get him to succumb to that fact, they could both be happy. Very happy.

"Please!" she screamed. She wrapped her arms around him, gripping tightly to his back.

"Now! Now, baby!" His demand came out at the same time he did. A powerful stream of semen shot into her, hot and searing, filling her until her own relief came from holding him, clutching him with arms and legs wound tight around him. The entire time, except for when she'd turned her head, he'd kept his gaze on hers, piercing her heart and soul.

She loved him.

Both panting, he lowered his body on top of hers. The crushing weight felt so good. Not smothering or overwhelming in any way. He was meant to be with her and she should be with him.

"I met this woman in a restaurant," Ned began softly, causing Fiona to raise an eyebrow. "She looked harmless." He cocked a smile. "So I followed her. We made love and she hurt me."

Her mouth dropped open. Before she could defend herself, he took her hand and placed it on his chest over his beating heart.

"Not here," he clarified. After giving her a quick peck, he eased off of her and sat on the bed with his back to her to show off eight red slits streaking horizontally across his lower back. Dumbstruck, Fiona hadn't realized she'd dug her fingernails into his flesh and hurt him. To Ned's credit, he hadn't screamed in pain or whimpered like she knew Kwame would have done.

"Guess I can't wear any backless dresses or halter tops either," he joked.

"I'm sorry I did that." Her fingertips danced over his flesh. His body flinched under her touch.

He turned to her. "I'm not. It's not a tattoo, but we both have something we went through tonight. We have battle scars to prove it."

Fortunately he didn't know about the scars around her heart, the wounds that started from her mother and continued with Kwame. And she couldn't let him know. He'd spent too much time worrying about her now. This was his time.

Ned fell back on the bed and curled his body next to hers. She tensed.

"Give me at least five minutes," she said, covering her chest.

A smile curled on his face as he curved his arm around her waist. How natural it felt. How comfortable.

Too comfortable.

"You'll be ready for round two in five?" he asked, nuzzling his face into her neck.

She bolted up. "No. I need to sleep in my own bed."

# *Chapter 11*

## *Pressing the flesh*

"Come on. Stay." Ned scurried to the edge of the bed, trying to capture Fiona's hand, an arm, her heart. But she was too fast. What had scared her so much?

"That's not the deal." She made it to the door but not before he jumped to his feet.

"Fuck the deal."

She flinched at how he said it. He couldn't tell if he'd scared her or excited her. He hoped the latter.

He continued. "You also said that we shouldn't kiss and we both agreed on no sex. Honey, we've already broken the deal eight ways to Sunday."

Her perfect, nude body whisked around his doorway, down the hall and into her room but not before he blocked her slamming the door by wedging his body between it and the jamb.

"What's so different now? It's not like you haven't slept in my bed before. Late night movies, thunderstorms..."

"Studying." Her gaze dropped to the floor as she backed away from him.

He felt like he was losing her and she was standing right in front of him. What did she want from him? What did she want, period? Did she want to still play the game?

Ned took a deep breath and crossed his arms. "As your doctor, I demand bed rest and constant supervision. I'll have to take your temperature every hour on the hour as well as a mammogram, Pap, and rectal exam. I wasn't able to get to that in this last session." He winked, hoping his false bravado and charm would be enough to get her back into bed.

He needed her next to him. Aside from making love to her and seeing her exquisite face when she came, memories that would be burned in his mind for a lifetime, he'd always wanted to wake up with her in his arms after making love.

Fiona smiled. His heart lifted and he fought to keep from beaming.

"That game is over, Neddy," she began. "You're a computer programmer. I'm," she gave a half laugh, "unemployed."

"You're more than that." He reached his hand out to her but she swatted it away, crushing his pounding heart like she'd stomped on it.

"I shouldn't be." She slid off the ring and placed it in his hand. "Relief, remember? That's what we're supposed to be to each other."

"Fine. Relieve me. I don't want to sleep alone tonight." Or ever, if he had his way. After setting the ring on her dresser, he stalked to her.

"What are you doing?" Her words came out like she was worried, but her expression betrayed her.

She looked excited. Her nipples puckered and it made him lick his tongue over his dry lips. She, in turn, licked her lips.

Her room already smelled like her sex, heady and sweet with a hint of vanilla and musk.

What he wanted from her was a night full of passion. He would hold her down and make slow love to her, then hot, pounding love, then he'd fold her in positions he'd only seen in the Kama Sutra. He would exhaust her so that she would have to sleep with him, no matter if it was in his bed or hers.

But once he looked into her eyes, his hand on the side of her face, something inside of him broke. The deeper he gazed, the more frightened she looked. It wasn't fear of what he would do to her. She knew that he would never harm her. But her eyes spoke of future terrors. *What would this do? What would happen to them? Would this be the end?*

He kissed her softly on the lips then turned to her door. With each step his raging hard-on deflated. After snatching his ring from the dresser, he muttered, "Good night," instead of his usual, "Love you like a rock." Then he closed her door.

* ~ *

Ned hated his job, and today people seemed to bother him more than usual. Why did they have to look at him that way? Damn it, did they all have to breathe?

Hell, it wasn't their fault. A rough night of dreaming about Fiona put him in the foulest of moods. The more he'd thought about making love to her to exhaustion, the worse he felt. He'd never thought he would use his best friend that way. How could he have thought of doing it last night?

He slammed his hand over a folder full of papers then punched some keys on his keyboard. When he felt a shaky hand touch his shoulder, Ned whipped his head around to find a sweaty, red-faced Fat Bastard staring back.

"Yes?" Ned asked.

"Uh," he pointed to Ned but looked too afraid of getting his name wrong this time. "Come with me to my office, son."

*Son.* That was a good cover. Ned locked his computer terminal and bolted up, causing Fat Bastard to stumble back when he towered over his boss. He followed the short, fat man down between the boxy, gray cubicles to Bastard's spacious, well-lit office.

Windows. *That's* what was missing from the office. They didn't have windows. Probably to keep the motley crew from taking a header twenty floors down.

Ned plopped down in a chair in front of Chunti's long, heavy mahogany desk. His eyes scanned the gold-plated nameplate, autographed baseball from Barry Bonds and open brochures for the newest Lexus convertible, not yet available in U.S. markets. Ned had done a little research himself. One of his many dream cars.

Chunti eased down into his burgundy leather swivel chair with a high back, then joined his hands together. "How are you doing?"

Ned sat up straighter to show some interest, but truly all he wanted to do was grab his stuff and go--where? He didn't want to go home. Fiona had his head so messed up, it no longer seemed like a sanctuary. *Did she want him or didn't she? Was this all for a promotion and letter or wasn't it? Was it real or was she faking it?*

Ned ground his teeth. "I'm fine, sir."

Chunti blinked. "You don't seem fine. As a matter of fact, your coworkers say you seem tense today. Any problems last night after dinner? Did you and Fiona get into a fight or something?"

Ned balled his hand into a fist but kept it from Chunti's view. It still bothered him that the man knew Fiona's name but not his.

"Or something," Ned replied.

Chunti shook his head. Ned imagined, though, that he was singing 'Hallelujah' in his mind and thinking this would be his way to getting to Fiona. That thought made him ball his other hand into a fist.

"You two are young. I'm sure you'll be able to work out your squabbles and get married."

"I don't know, sir. I don't see marriage in the cards for us."

Chunti looked more disappointed than his mother had when he'd told her about their scheme.

"Oh no! But you two seemed so happy together," Fat Bastard said.

"Well, it happens." Ned stood, not wanting to discuss his personal life any further. He should have just smiled, nodded and accepted everything Chunti had to say. "Can I get back to work now?"

"No, sir. As a matter of fact," Fat Bastard cranked up to his feet in a slow, dramatic way, "I want you to take the rest of the day off."

It was already noon. He would have had three hours left in his day. Big whoop.

"That's not necessary, sir. I can finish out my day. I promise to be better tomorrow."

"No, I insist. I want you two happy when you come to my house this Saturday." He put his hand on Ned's back and ushered him to his door.

Ned kept his eyes on the short man, furrowing his eyebrows when he saw how extremely happy Chunti got after opening his office door.

"Looks like your fiancée wants the same thing." Chunti pointed toward Ned's workstation where he saw a group of men swarming his area and a pair of golden brown legs poking between them.

Ned wanted to be mad. But seeing as this was the first time Fiona had ever come to his place of work and knowing how much he'd wanted to see her, how could he?

"I apologize, sir. I know your policy on guests in the workplace. I'll get rid of her and get back to work." He started for the group but was halted by Chunti's fat fingers around his arm.

"No apologies necessary. Take your beautiful fiancée home and you two make up. I'll see you bright and early in the morning, and that's an order."

Ned nodded and broke free from Chunti's grip. Each step he took toward her, his heart pounded in double time. What was she doing here? With Fiona, it could be for any reason.

As he got closer, he heard the men around her laughing. That Fiona. His Fiona. What a charmer. Breaking through the crowd, Ned came face to face with his faux intended.

Fiona sat poised in his chair holding up her picture. Her smile lit the clan of men around her. If she only knew the power she wielded, she would use it for evil and not ... well, then again, what she was doing was pretty evil. Nasty. Dirty. Ned clasped his hands in front of his swelling erection and plastered a smile on his face.

"Hi, honey," she said.

Although Fiona didn't have on the hair extension she'd had last night, she was wearing a wig. She almost looked like she did in high school and college. The wig was long and brown, almost a honey blond. It cascaded in big curls down around her face. And in her white halter top and matching short, pleated skirt, there was no way she blended in with the crowd. She meant to stand out and be noticed.

"Hi." Ned scanned the men who all seemed oblivious that he was standing there. They kept their gazes trained on Fiona.

"I was just telling your coworkers about this picture." She held up the frame. "Cancun. Hot beaches. Even hotter nights."

The men chuckled. The women close by clicked their tongues. Ned busied himself by trying to log off of his computer and get his things before Fiona caused a riot.

"We didn't know you had it in you, buddy," Nose-Picker said.

Ned nodded as he locked his desk, gathered his CDs and threw them in his briefcase.

"Yeah, where have you been hiding this beautiful creature?" Smells Like Pot asked.

"Honey, you haven't been talking a blue streak about me?" Fiona pouted.

Ned wanted to hurl. She was going overboard with the sex kitten act. Where was his smart, beautiful, no-nonsense best friend and why was this bimbo pretending to be her? Last night she looked terrified to have him spend the night in her bedroom. What had changed?

"Surprise, surprise." He grabbed her arm and brought her to her feet. "I actually work when I'm here instead of gossiping."

He surveyed the men's expressions. Some looked as shocked as if he'd accused them of murder. The others acted as though Ned was committing murder when he pulled Fiona away from the group.

"See y'all tomorrow."

"What?" Fiona asked.

Ned kept talking as he headed her to the elevator. "Chunti gave me the rest of the day off. By the way, why are you here?"

Since Ned held her upper arm, Fiona managed to wrap her arm around Ned's back. "I heard you slamming things around this morning before you left for work. So I packed you a lunch."

Ned scanned her. Purse small enough to keep a Tic Tac. Nothing but luscious tits in her halter. Not even a visible panty line under her skirt.

"Where's the lunch? In your hair?" he asked when they got to the elevator.

"Better. In the car."

"Mmm, sounds good. I hope in this heat you brought egg salad sandwiches and potato salad and you have them packed in the trunk. I've always wanted food poisoning for lunch."

"Ha, ha."

The elevator doors opened and the duo stepped inside as soon as two people stepped out.

"I guess Mr. Chunti noticed you were a little tense too." Fiona wiped her hand down his lapels.

One man in the car with them turned slightly to catch the sight of her, then looked away with a small smile. Ned's heart pounded in his ears. The man was jealous of Ned because of Fiona's attention.

"Yeah, he said we should make up," Ned said in an intimate manner.

Fiona blinked. "So you're still upset about last night?"

This time all three of the other passengers turned to look at them. Ned felt their stares and sweat formed above his eyebrows. The elevator stopped and two of them got off. Ned wanted them all gone.

"Can we talk about this in the car?" Ned asked between gritted teeth.

That made Fiona smile even wider. "Sure. As long as you don't try to do that thing you did the other night when we were going down the interstate." She tapped the end of his nose. "I swear I thought we were going to crash right before you ca..."

"Whoa!" Ned cut her off before she could further incriminate him. "This is our stop."

"The fourteenth floor?" Fiona questioned. "But we need to..."

Ned pulled her from the elevator and found the stairs. As soon as got her inside of the stairwell, he laid into her.

"What the hell are you doing? I have to work with these people. I don't want them thinking I'm some sort of sex-fiend pervert," Ned hissed, standing a step lower than Fiona.

"Come on. Loosen up, Neddy." Her pouty sex kitten act dropped away. "The whole idea was to have your coworkers see us together. None of them will see me when you go to the barbeque. Only the VP's. So now everyone knows you're a stud."

Ned snorted and headed down the stairs. "God, sometimes I could just put you over my knee and..."

"And what?"

Ned halted, pivoting to catch a defiant-looking Fiona still standing on the top step, her arms crossed.

"What? You want to spank me?" she asked.

"I was kidding. You're acting like a kid right now. All these secrets and lies. I don't like it." He ran his fingers through his hair. "Let's just go home."

"No." Fiona dropped her purse to the floor and started lifting her skirt. "I have been a very, very bad girl. I think I deserve a spanking."

"Don't do that." He rushed to her. "There are cameras everywhere." With a slight head nod to the upper corner of the empty stairwell, he got Fiona to look up to see the small red light above the camera lens.

When she turned back to him she said, "Perfect. We'll fuck in the stairwell and get more people talking than when Paris Hilton videotaped herself and her man having sex."

"That'll be a boon for your law career."

"Why do you think I'm wearing a wig? Besides, no one in there knows my last name."

"Chunti knows you're with me. He watches these tapes like amateur porno. I'm not subjecting you to that."

Fiona bit back a smile. Ned was so protective of her. It was amazing. But he was so careful. That wouldn't do for a man looking to move up in business.

She pulled down her skirt and picked up her purse. "Fine. You win, Sensible Neddy." She followed him down the remaining fourteen flights of stairs. At the bottom, when they crashed through the door leading to the parking garage, Fiona said, "I wish sometimes you could be a little adventurous."

"I'm friends with you. Isn't that adventurous enough?" He followed her to her car.

When she opened the door, smells of fried chicken, corn on the cob and sweet cinnamon barreled out. Ned inhaled deeply, then smiled.

"You weren't kidding about lunch."

"That's the other thing I don't mess around with. You don't joke about The Force and don't kid about food."

He helped her into her car. "Follow me."

"Where are we going?" she asked.

"Now where's *your* sense of adventure?" He winked, then ran over to his car.

*Adventure and Ned?* Fiona had to see this for herself.

# *Chapter 12*

## *Choose your words carefully*

Ned drove to a park close to their apartment building. The whole trip over, which took about fifteen minutes, he thought about Fiona's hands lifting her skirt on the stairs. Another inch and he would have seen heaven.

Oh, how he'd wanted her so much then. His dick had nearly burst through his pants as he thought about ripping her panties down and burying his face between her legs, inhaling that sweet scent of hers and tasting her nectar.

With her short pleated skirt and her hair color almost like when she was in high school, she looked like the untouchable cheerleader he would sneak peeks at when he first arrived at Clinton High School.

But he had to be level-headed and think about her needs instead of his own. She wanted a career in law. She deserved a career. He didn't want it ruined by giving his boss and the security guards a peep show. But her claim that he wasn't adventurous stuck in his mind. He'd prove to her he *was*.

Ned tried not to be the person defined by others. His classmates had all called him a nerd, a loser, a nobody. He carried those harsh words around with him like a necklace that choked him.

Ned parked by the picnic area next to a table. Fiona parked her car next to his.

"Did you bring a blanket or tablecloth?" he asked when she got out of her car.

She winced. "I knew there was one thing I was forgetting."

"Don't worry. I have a blanket in the car."

"Good ol' reliable Ned. You're like a regular Boy Scout, you know that?"

After retrieving the black-and-red checkered blanket with tasseled edges, he said, "So I've been told."

He selected a spot by the water and spread the blanket under a tree. The location was perfect. The sun chandeliered over them, emitting buttery-gold rays of light. But the tree he chose to set up under shielded them. He didn't even plan it. And with the slight breeze, it made sitting outside tolerable.

Ned helped spread out the food. Once everything was set, Fiona kicked off her shoes and sat on it Indian style. After removing his jacket, tie and long-sleeved shirt, Ned, also, took off his shoes and socks, and sat next to her in his T-shirt and dress slacks.

"Show me what you got," Ned said and rubbed his hands together.

"I tried doing that earlier but you stopped me." She winked as she brought around the large wicker basket.

Her response made him blink. "What are you doing?"

Setting out plates, she kept her gaze from him. "What?"

"This whole come-fuck-me attitude. I don't get it."

"Oh, I think you've been getting it right regularly for a couple of days now." She snickered.

"There you go again. We don't have to keep going on the physical part of the plan. Chunti thinks we're a couple. Thanks to your little show, my coworkers think we're a couple. It won't be difficult to convince Kristoff. So if you want to stop, we can. It'll be hard."

"It will?" She placed her hand on his crotch. "Hmm, I can feel that."

He held her wrist and, while repeating a boatload of 'Hail Marys' in his head, removed her hand from his throbbing penis. "Talk to me, Fi. Have I fucked up somewhere? Are you pissed off at me?"

After pulling her arm away she laughed off his questions. "No. Why would I be mad at you? Chicken?"

He blinked again because she'd said 'chicken' like it was his name and not what was on the lunch menu. She placed a large breast on his plate.

"I don't know," he began. "But I don't get why you're acting like this."

"I'm not doing anything. Cornhead? I mean cornbread." She snickered again as she gave him a delectable square of bread.

Now *that* name was deliberate.

"I'm not using you for sex." He wanted her to be clear on what he was thinking.

"I know. We've talked about that, remember? Fruit?"

His eyes widened. "You think I'm gay?"

"Of course not. Where would you get that idea?"

"You've been calling me names since we sat down."

He picked up his breast and took a healthy chomp from it. If the damn meat didn't melt in his mouth and taste so good, he would have been mad at her. But the woman cooked like an angel.

"What names?" she asked, innocence personified.

"Oh, I don't know. Chicken. Cornhead. Fruit."

She held up a container. After popping open the lid, she showed him the contents. "Strawberries. They're in season. Thought you'd like some with whipped cream."

Squinting his eye, he stared at her. "What? No cream puff jokes?"

"Thought it'd be too easy. Couldn't think of what else to say."

"Ah ha!" He slammed down his breast and grabbed her shoulders, pinning her to the ground and straddling her body. "So you *are* taking little digs at me."

"Okay, let me up, Neddy. You're being ridiculous." Her body squirmed under him.

The grinding felt oh so good against his dick, still looking for some attention since she'd put her hand on it moments before.

Remember, Ned, you're supposed to be mad at her. So stop popping a woody.

"*I'm* being ridiculous? You've been calling me names. You're being childish and even worse, you won't tell me why."

"You're getting grease on me. If you mess up this outfit..."

"Tell me why you're mad. Is it Kristoff?"

"Always." She thrashed her body about, kicking her feet. Thank God the park rangers weren't around. They would have arrested him for assault.

"Is it your mom?" he asked.

"Duh. But I can handle her." Flailing her arms, she pounded the ground in frustration.

"Is it me?"

That's when she stopped. She brought her gaze to his and stared. Ned felt his heart slowing down until he thought it would stop completely, killing him on the spot while he waited for her answer.

But as he watched her, looking into her eyes, seeing the golden flecks reflected in her green eyes courtesy of the beaming sun, he noticed her face soften. She took in a deep breath and waited a beat before letting it out. It was in her exhalation that it hit Ned.

Leaning back on his haunches, he let her go. "My feelings haven't changed about you," he began. "Have yours about me?"

When she didn't answer right away, he squeezed his eyes shut and hoped for a quick end to this torture.

"Stop getting that worried look on your face, Ned." She glanced away for a moment, eyeing the still pond.

Her life matched the pond. Still. Quiet. Nothing going on. Meanwhile Ned was on the fast track to a great new career. And she certainly could be as well ... a career she knew she would hate.

"You always could read me like a book." He hopped off of her and retrieved his plate before any ants could get their sights on it.

"It's me." She sat up.

While wiping off her top and skirt, she kept her gaze on the pool of water, not wanting to face her friend. How could she? If she admitted that she didn't want to work in law at all, that it was her mom's dream and not hers, Ned would be angry and probably break off their friendship. She'd seen how upset he'd gotten when she'd set up the dinner plans with Chunti. And when he found out she'd told Chunti they were engaged, she thought he would blow his top.

But she'd never really expected for him to agree to this plan. She thought if she threw another obstacle in her way, then it would give her a perfect out, a great excuse for not getting the clerk's position in Kristoff's court. But ol' Agreeable Ned, never one to turn her down, as usual stepped up to the plate. Never one to disappoint. And he hadn't.

On so many levels he had pleased her. Sexually, emotionally. How could she tell him that her life plans didn't involve her becoming a lawyer, let alone a judge? He would think she was still the bubble-headed cheerleader she used to be.

She wanted so much to impress him still.

"Earth to Fi." He snapped his fingers in her face.

Fiona blinked before returning her gaze to his.

"Before you spaced out you said something about you having a problem with yourself. What is it?" He finished off his chicken breast in record time and was working on a second one, which was why she'd made a whole tray just for him. She knew what he liked and how to make it.

"I was just wondering what I should wear to the barbeque on Saturday," she hedged.

Ned screwed up his face, making it apparent that he knew she'd lied. "We talked about this before. Come on, Fi. Fess up. What's really going on?"

She sighed and on the exhale said, "What I'm worried about is that you're going to eat all of the food before I get any."

Before he could further question her, she grabbed a plate and loaded chicken, corn and cornbread on it. She would *have* to tell Ned about how she really felt about pursuing a career in law after the barbeque. Maybe a good discussion with Kristoff would change her mind. Maybe.

Ned stared at the back of his hand as he reclined, resting on one elbow on top of the blanket. He never noticed the scratch that went down his middle finger. Even if he didn't know the back of his hand, he knew Fiona like no one else did.

The woman was hiding something from him. He knew it. He felt it. It was the way she avoided looking at him and how she fidgeted with her clothes. It was the same feeling he'd gotten the night she'd run from his bedroom, refusing to sleep there with him. It was as though half of her wanted to be close and intimate but the other half didn't. It didn't make any sense.

What was she keeping from him? Maybe she'd planned on going back to her parents after all. She couldn't. Not now. Not after all they've done.

God, what they've done. If he were his old self, he would have blushed. But she'd changed him. Man, how she changed him. He hungered for her touch, her smell, to hear her moan and call his name.

Too bad it was all an act, a game to trick his boss and fool Kristoff.

As he watched her next to him on the blanket, staring out at the water and occasionally throwing rocks into it to make the surface ripple, he smiled. Sitting here like this reminded him so much of when they were in high school and would go behind the school to the lake and tell secrets to each other.

Fiona was all together strong but so soft and innocent. A beautiful woman with a heart of gold. And what was he? A doofus with two left feet, no ability to fight and a nowhere job. So naturally when she came up with this ridiculous plan to play boyfriend and girlfriend he thought she'd lost her mind. But to actually go through it, to feel her, touch her, have her look at him like he was the only person in the world to matter to her, made him feel like King Kong.

But when all of the games and the charades were said and done, what would happen to them?

Maybe that's what Fiona had been pondering since they came to the park for lunch. She was probably coming up with a way to let him down easy. Thinking up ways to say good-bye before the barbeque. God, he had to get ahead at work if he wanted to keep Fi in his life. Maybe he would be more tolerable to be with if he had a better job making more money. Fiona deserved to be with a successful man. All gorgeous women were built that way. Hell, even if Fiona didn't take his breath away every time he looked at her, she would have still deserved the best in life.

His friend was smart. Super talented. She could do anything she wanted including being a supreme court judge. He could see her sitting on the bench, handing down decisions in that black robe. Maybe completely naked under the robe.

Ned rubbed his eyes. He had to stop thinking of his best friend as a sex object. She was certainly more than that to him. And if she was planning to leave him, he had to show her at least one last time just how much she meant to him.

Sliding over to her, his gaze never left her face, bathed in the glow of the afternoon sun. Her skin radiated as though she shouldn't be touched. But that made him want to caress her more.

His hand slid over her naked thigh. He couldn't discern whether the sun had baked her or if she was naturally this warm. Whatever it was, the feeling left him hungering for more. He snaked his other hand around her waist until his head rested on her lap.

She stroked his hair as she had done a million times before. But now it seemed like it would be her last time making this kind and cozy gesture. He nuzzled his head against her stomach.

"What are you doing?" she whispered but didn't move, didn't stop stroking his hair, which had to have been wet with sweat from sitting in the humid heat.

"Isn't this what couples do after a big, satisfying meal? Don't they clean up and cuddle?" he asked.

Not a scrap of food remained after they'd eaten lunch so the only clean up they'd had to do consisted of putting the basket and the utensils in the car.

"Some couples." Her hand drifted down his neck to his shoulder, then lower each time she stroked his hair.

"Would we be that type of couple?" He lifted his head and turned his gaze up so that he could look her in her eyes.

"Probably," she said. "You know how much I like to play with your hair."

He glanced over her shoulder as though he saw someone or something, then directed his attention back to her. "Maybe we should kiss."

She swallowed. Not that her Nice Neddy had made her nervous. But she didn't know if she could keep the excited look off her face. She'd been thinking since they'd sat down for lunch how she would tell him how she really felt about pursuing a law career. But for now, now that she had this wonderful, caring and sincere man in her arms, she wanted nothing more than to make the moment last.

"Yeah, if anyone from work is around, they'll need to see us being..."

He cut her off. "Intimate."

She nodded.

Before she knew it or could anticipate it, Ned's firm lips covered hers in what started as a sweet kiss but gradually, almost without notice, turned into something more passionate. He leaned into her, making her recline back until she lay flat on her back.

Cupping the back of his head, she brought him in, encouraging him to continue. Her other hand stroked his back as he moved over her, pressing his body onto hers until she felt breathless, not because of his weight but because his tender kiss stole her breath.

His tongue probed her mouth and she happily accepted it, sucking it as though it contained sustenance to fuel her body. He tasted of summer in the south, sweet chicken meat, creamy butter and strawberries all rolled into a wonderful concoction that only existed in his mouth. Thank goodness she didn't bring the peaches. She would have been a goner!

Her hand fisted his hair in the back of his head as her legs looped around his body. She felt his heartbeat increase in its pounding until the hammering beat against her own chest. His large hand cradled the back of her head and the other hand roamed over her breasts.

Too much. Her nipples responded by hardening to an aching degree, pressing against the fabric of her top. Her thong had to be a soaking patch and string by now.

Ned broke from the kiss but kept his head hovering above hers. "We're supposed to be engaged, right?"

Again, Fiona nodded. She didn't trust herself to speak.

"And we're in love?"

She didn't know about Ned, but she knew she had fallen for him. Head over heels. It wasn't supposed to have been part of the plan. But she was in way over her head and didn't know how to get out.

"Supposed to be," she finally answered, her voice squeaking for good measure.

Ned started fiddling with the clasp behind her halter top at her back. "I think it's time we do something creative. If we get caught, it'll be more proof that we are who we are."

"And if we don't get caught?"

He stopped for a moment. A smile crept up. "Let's just hope we get caught." Then he winked.

Nice Ned turned into Naughty Ned with a blink of an eye. She liked that. He was a man full of surprises.

When he couldn't work her clasp, she stopped him with a hand on his shoulder. "It's still so early out," she began. "Maybe someone will see us. Kids. We *are* in a park."

"So who's the chicken now?" He smirked. Before she could respond, he looked over his shoulder then directed his attention to her again. "I have an idea."

He sprang to his feet, held out his hand for her and helped her to stand. With a subtle gesture, he directed her to get off of the blanket. After hopping off, he shook out the leaves, grass, twigs and anything else that managed to latch itself to the fabric.

What her eyes couldn't stop staring at was the bulge in his pants. She licked her lips and hoped that Ned could maintain that healthy hard-on until they got home. She guessed he had gathered the blanket to fold and get them out of there.

Instead he took her hand and led her behind a large, wide tree. Facing the lake, he sat with his back against the tree.

"Sit on my lap." He held his arms out.

With the welcoming look in his eyes and the way her pussy throbbed, she didn't second guess him. She eased down on him, her butt pressed firmly against his hardness. She twirled her hips for good measure and got rewarded with a low groan. But when he threw the blanket over her lap she shook her head.

"It's too hot." She attempted to pull the wool throw off her but Ned secured it tightly around her waist and his.

"Don't worry. I'll make it worth the inconvenience. Just hold it up."

She did so and felt his hands under her butt. He cupped it, squeezing it and massaging it until she leaned her head back against him. She closed her eyes and gripped the blanket, unaware of what to do with her hands.

He molded her like a chef would knead pizza dough. Cupping her, grabbing her, squeezing until he got the right response.

When he stopped and she felt him fidgeting under her, tugging her thong to the side, her eyes popped open. Surely he wasn't about to make love to her in broad daylight in the park?

Before she completed her thought, she felt his thick mushroom tip pushing against her opening until, with her downward grind and his thrust, he pushed all the way inside of her.

They both let out small cries as her bare feet planted against the earth and his hands gripped her hips as he made small thrusts in and out of her. So easy were the movements that he felt like a part of her, like a steady heartbeat.

His soft lips kissed her shoulder, then he licked the spot, cooling it, while the rest of her body went up in flames. The blanket on her lap had nothing to do with the heat and had everything to do with this sexy, *adventurous* man underneath her, making love to her in the park, making her feel wanted, needed, special.

She didn't care if anyone walked by at that moment. The time was theirs. This belonged to them. This man was hers. And whether she wanted to admit it or not, she loved him. Loved him like a friend, loved him like a lover, loved every part of him.

But maybe this physical relationship was the last thing she could enjoy with him. Once he found out her deception, she was sure he would hate her, throw her out of his place, and never speak to her again.

"Oh, Ned!" she cried, overcome both at the thought of losing him and by his lovemaking making her feel so incredible. She didn't want to think about what could happen. She wanted to embrace what he was doing to her now.

His pulsating penis filled her until she had to reach behind herself and grip the back of his head. Twining his arms around her waist, he held her like he never wanted to let her go. She spread her legs under the blanket and ground herself on him until she couldn't differentiate between the sound of the water lapping against the edge and the juices from her pussy sliding up and down his shaft.

Raising his hips from the ground, he moved in and out of her faster until Fiona felt as though she were floating. The pressure built inside of her as her body trembled. He must have felt her because he made one deep penetrating thrust before completely blowing her mind by pounding her hard with quick plunges.

He moaned so loudly that a squirrel close by scurried away and up a tree. She was sure she'd pulled out a section of his hair when her orgasm hit her at about the same time. Lowering them back down to the ground, Ned kept her still close to him.

Breathlessly, he said, "If I were to die at this moment..."

She cut him off. "Don't say that. That's so bad to think, let alone say."

But he kept on. "If I die right now, I would be a happy fucking man."

She didn't want to hear him say that, but she couldn't help but smile. "Really?"

He kissed the back of her neck, put his finger to her chin and turned her face around to his. "Hell, yes. I fulfilled one of my fantasies."

She smiled wider. "You did?"

He nodded. "Yep. I fucked a cheerleader-prom queen in the great outdoors."

Her smile slid down her face like melting ice cream. Most people smoke after sex. Fiona fumed.

# *Chapter 13*

## *Expect the unexpected*

Ned had fucked up. He messed up big time and it had everything to do with his big mouth.

After their incredible lovemaking session in the park, he'd made the monumental mistake of reducing the whole thing to just a fantasy moment with Fiona's old self. *Of course* she meant more than that to him. But he couldn't tell her. How was some computer geek and former high school nerd supposed to tell this dream woman that he was deeply in love with her? She would have laughed at him like other people had in high school.

Who was he kidding? Fiona wouldn't have done that. She'd never laughed at him, not even in high school. She was about the only one, too. Certainly in these last few days, she'd never laughed at their lovemaking sessions. So why had he said such a stupid thing?

Fear. Had to be. If she was going to leave him soon, then he wanted to be as unaffected as possible. The best way to do that was to see her as a caricature. Only problem was that he loved her too damn much.

Ned glanced at his watch again. Fiona had been tight-lipped since their picnic. He still remembered her getting off of his lap in a quick jolt, leaving his happy johnson to swing in the open air as she straightened her short skirt and stomped to her car without a word. Regret still plagued him as he stood outside of her bedroom door.

She hadn't mentioned the barbeque, and whether she'd changed her mind about going. He hoped she hadn't. But he'd been too afraid to ask. If they were going, they had thirty minutes to get there. And he still didn't know if she was planning to go with him, or if she'd even gotten dressed for it.

Ned took a deep breath, curled his fingers into a weak fist and raised his hand to the door ... and held it there, not moving. *Come on, man. She's your friend. What can she do to you?* Well, for starters, she could tell him to go to hell and never speak to him again. It was bad enough that her look had already said that.

He cleared his throat and made a light rap on her door. "Fi, are you up?" he asked, his voice as light as the knock. "If we're going to the picnic, we have to leave now. Chunti's a stickler for people who arrive late."

Nothing. Not a sound. Not a movement. Maybe she was sleeping.

He knocked again, harder this time. "Come on, Fi. I told you I was sorry. I shouldn't have said what I said that day. You did a great thing for me by bringing out lunch. And afterward when we..." He hesitated, pressing his hand against her cool door as though he could feel her through it. "I've never felt so wonderful in my life." If he was going to get her out, he knew there was only one way to do it. He had to tell her the truth. He loved her. Loved her with all of his geeky heart. It pained him that she had been so hurt by something he'd said. He'd never wanted to hurt her. Ever. "Fiona, I..."

Before he could get out his declaration, her door finally swung open. She wore a white sleeveless mock-turtleneck top, white slacks and white strappy sandals. A harsh expression masked her face. She looked more like the hard-ass attorney she aspired to be than his soft, beautiful Fiona with a heart as big as the first computer ever built.

Even her normally soft curly hair had been pulled back into a severe looking bun. The only makeup she wore was a dramatic red lipstick that made her juicy lips look like she'd drank blood for breakfast and needed another feed soon.

"Ready?" It was the first word she'd said to him in two days.

"Uh, yeah. You know when I said you should wear a turtleneck and pants to the picnic, I was kidding."

He peered over her shoulder into her room and saw a set of suitcases sitting next to her bed. His eyes widened.

She slammed her door before he could say anything. "Let's go. A promise is a promise. I won't let you down."

Fiona stomped toward the door, grabbing her purse along the way.

"Fi, would you stop for a second. We should talk before we go."

"No, I think you've said enough." She opened the door, then did something he didn't think she would be capable of doing since he caught foot-in-mouth disease. She craned up a phony smile that would rival any politician's. "Besides, I used to be a cheerleader and a prom queen. I'll just cheer you on to victory. Go, Neddy!" She even topped her bitter speech with her hands in the air, just like she would do when she was leading a cheer.

"Wait." He reached for her but she slipped away from his grasp.

"Don't want to be late."

He suspected as far as apologies were concerned, he was too late for that too.

* ~ *

Fiona remained quiet the entire trip to Chunti's home. Keeping her arms crossed over her chest, she was fixated on the scenery rushing by. All of her plans were falling down around her like a house of cards.

First she tried being the perfect daughter by going into a respected field she knew her mother would love and would shock her critics. She didn't want to be thought as the vacuous, dim cheerleader. But everything she'd said and done proved her detractors right. First by hiding her true passions and interests, even from herself, then coming up with that plan of acting like a couple with Ned just to satisfy her physical needs.

No, the plan was for more than that.

She'd loved Ned since she saw him walking in to his desk that first day in French class.

Turning her head now to steal a quick glance at him, she had to turn away as soon as she caught his blue-eyed gaze staring back.

"We're almost there," he said.

She nodded in response but resumed watching the ever-changing scenery.

How could she have treated Ned this way? He didn't deserve to be used. She winced when she thought about the cheerleader-prom queen crack he'd made after they'd made love. Not that she could blame him.

She *had* acted immature. She'd been angry with herself and took it out on him by calling him names. Cornhead. She squeezed a disapproving noise through her nose that got his attention.

"Did you say something?" he asked.

She didn't answer, keeping her gaze trained to the window. Her hand smoothed over her white slacks. Even thought they were cool, she would have happier wearing shorts or a skirt.

What was she trying to prove with this outfit? Then again, what was she trying to prove wearing the white halter outfit the other day? She shook her head when she realized how much her pleated skirt looked like her old cheerleading skirt. No wonder Ned had said what he did. Her old persona was safe, easy to revert back to when real life got too complicated, too real. The sad part though was that she'd hoped Ned would be the one person who would have seen past all of that. But then again how could she blame him? She couldn't shake the stigma even years later.

When he didn't recognize Fiona's true self, when he called her a cheerleader, she realized that no matter what she did in life, she would always be that to him. He would never take her seriously. How could he, when she was hiding so many parts of herself? If he couldn't, then the people around him wouldn't take *him* seriously. Fiona never factored in the backlash Ned could get because of the company he kept. Would they think less of him because he seemed so shallow? Even if she couldn't figure out what to do with her life, she couldn't drag Ned down with her.

So she'd called her mom after their disastrous lunch and asked if she could move back home. She would tell Ned after the barbeque. He would hate her but at least she wouldn't be there to see the disappointment in his eyes.

That would hurt more than to see those bright blue eyes look clouded over with sadness and anger. One thing she had to do before breaking their union, dissolving their friendship, was reveal the truth, truth about her passion for the career she really wanted and the passion in her heart for him. He would laugh at her but at least he would finally know the truth.

Ned pulled up the long driveway that led to Chunti's estate. A guard met them and cleared them to proceed. The slow ascent to the front of Chunti's home allowed Fiona to take a few deep breaths and muster some strength to tell Ned what plagued her heart and her soul.

"Ned," she began.

Splitting his attention between the valet directing him to a spot and her, he volleyed his head back and forth. "What, Fi?"

Her mouth opened but nothing came out until she put her hand on her stomach as though having to push the air out of her mouth to form words. "We need to talk," she finally managed.

Ned parked and turned the car off before she'd gotten the last word out. "What? I'm all ears. You want to leave here and go back home? I'll turn us around. You want to go inside and have me be the perfect fiancé to Chunti and Kristoff, I'm willing to do that too. Tell me what you want. Tell me what's on your mind."

Her throat tightened and before she could get a word out, both of their doors opened, Chunti on Ned's side and a woman who looked like a female version of him on Fiona's side. Sister, maybe?

"Nelly! You made it!" Chunti grabbed Ned's hand and pulled him out of the car.

"And you must be Fiona!" the woman exclaimed, with an equally forceful maneuver to haul Fiona from the car.

Ned slammed his car door as the fat bastard pumped his hand up and down. He couldn't tell if it was the heat that made his face and neck feel so hot or the anger that boiled in him when Chunti pulled him away from the woman who he cared about more than his own miserable life. She wanted to talk, about what he wasn't sure. But it was a start.

"How are you, boy?" Fat Bastard asked.

"I would be doing better, sir, if you could call me by my real name."

He was over the pleasantries. How much shit did he have to eat? When he turned his gaze to Fiona and the woman who had apprehended her and caught their shocked expressions, he realized very quickly why he was still chewing on his shit sandwich.

Fiona.

So he quickly plastered a smile on his face and squeezed Fat Bastard's hand. "Ned. The name's Ned Cholurski, and I'm sure Fiona and I will have a great time here."

A slow smile curled up his round pie face. "I'm sorry, son." He leaned in. "Already had a nip before the guests arrived."

Yes, because Ned couldn't tell that already from the stench from his breath and a red bulbous nose that would make Rudolph the Red-Nosed Reindeer jealous. The man smelled like a walking distillery. His insides must be pickled.

Chunti grabbed Ned's shoulder and turned him around. "That there is the missus, Charley."

Charley Chunti. What a bad hand to be dealt with in life to end up falling in love and marrying a man who would have her name changed to Charley Chunti.

"Most of my friends call me C.C." She made her way around the front of his car, pulling Fiona behind her. "I've met your lovely fiancée. What did you say your name is, baby?"

Her southern drawl was thick enough to spread on buttermilk biscuits and make honey seem like a quick-pouring liquid.

"Ned. Ned Cholurski." He shook her fingertips, the only thing the woman allowed him to take when she extended her hand.

A short, round woman with a cotton candy-like, poofed out, blonde Afro of a hairdo, Ned hadn't pictured this robust woman to be a delicate, shrinking violet. Guess he didn't know everything, something he'd tried to explain to Fiona yesterday and all that morning but she wouldn't hear of it.

Other cars pulled in around them as the Chuntis led Ned and Fiona up to the house. Ned tried to respond to the banal conversation Fat Bastard tried to strike up, but all his attention went to the woman in white, his angel, who right now looked uncomfortable and unhappy.

"Sir, do you have a bathroom that we could use?" Ned asked, trying to figure a way to be alone with Fiona. "Maybe we could freshen up a little."

"Sure, sure!" Fat Bastard gave him another slap on his back.

Ned smiled.

"But later," Chunti said.

Ned frowned.

"I have some people for you to meet. Unless you've been doing something in the car that you don't want me and the missus to know about, then I'd say you're pretty clean." Chunti winked.

Ned's stomach tightened and he had to swallow to keep his breakfast from ending up on this toad's face and evenly manicured lawn.

"Let me give you a tour of the house," C.C. said to Fiona.

She pulled his Fiona one way and Chunti pulled him another way. This would be a long, long day.

\* ~ \*

How could Fiona have been so stupid? She should have told Ned how she felt way before they got to the house and before they both got pulled from the car like they were criminals.

Although a bit brusque, C.C. seemed friendly. She showed Fiona around the expansive house, pointing out special places and pictures. She showed off photos of her grandchildren, her seven children, all successful of course, and their prized horses.

Amazing. Such a lavish home. It reeked of the riches Chunti had made. But clearly what mattered most to this woman was her family. In a crystal picture frame, she showed off her favorite pooch, a toy poodle named Toy. No imagination there.

In an antique armoire, she pointed to the homemade ashtrays her children had made when they were in grade school, wobbly, ill-shaped monstrosities that sat next to Ming vases and expensive busts.

"So how long will you wait after you and Ned marry until you'll be having children?" C.C. inquired as casually as if she'd asked Fiona if Fiona had enjoyed the tour of the home.

Fiona blinked and focused on the woman. Should she be honest and crush the woman's spirit, thereby also ruining Ned's chance at getting promoted? With seven children and countless grandchildren, it was apparent that Chunti put a high value on family even though the guy came off as a creep. Or should Fiona tell C.C. what she wanted to hear, that she couldn't wait to start a family and better yet, she might be carrying a little something inside of her now.

No, that was what had gotten her in trouble in the first place. The lies, the deception, the stories. She had to be honest. And honestly it shouldn't matter what she and Ned did in life. What should matter was his incredible talent.

"I don't want children, Mrs. Chunti." Fiona attempted to walk away, but C.C. took her hand in a grip even stronger than her handshake, and pulled Fiona back to capture her gaze.

"What? Are you not able to have children, baby?" she asked, her drawl becoming considerably slower.

"I didn't say I couldn't have children. I don't *want* children." She tried extracting her hand from the woman's grasp but C.C. clamped down tighter. It was apparent she would make it her mission to convince Fiona of the errors of her ways for not wanting to bring forth life, be fruitful and multiply, as it were.

"That's just silly. You're a beautiful girl. That Ned's a handsome man. You two would have beautiful babies. Look at that Halle Berry. Beautiful biracial woman."

Great. Now she and Ned had the responsibility of bringing more beautiful biracial children in the world.

"I want to concentrate on my career. I couldn't devote the time needed to raise a child." Part of that was the truth. She wanted to concentrate on a career, though not necessarily law. And she really didn't have the time needed to raise a child. Couldn't this woman be thankful that Fiona was responsible enough to know she didn't want to have children, that she thought it was better left to those who actively wanted to be parents, instead of being unsure and bringing a child into the world and ruining it, possibly raising the next serial killer?

"Hogwash!"

Guess not.

C.C. continued, "When me and Frank married, we couldn't wait to start a family. And at the time we got married, I was the one with the career. You think Frank's work at Meta Corporation bought this house and everything you see in it?" She shook her head. "We call that play money."

Fiona wanted to ask if she could play in that money.

"I bred horses when I was sixteen. Invested well. Then I came up with a shampoo to detangle their manes and tails when I was eighteen. Sold it to a corporation where I'm still a managing partner. Invested well. Then I wrote a book on throwing a wonderful, southern dinner party before that Martha Stewart woman did. It sold very well. And, again, I invested well. All of this before I said 'I do' and started having children at the ripe old age of twenty-two."

"That was great for you, C.C. You had your career, or rather careers, before you got married and had a family. I don't have that."

She covered Fiona's hand and looked into her eyes as though she were going to share the secret of life. "Don't you see, baby? I would have given all of that up for my family. Essentially, I did. As soon as I got pregnant, I stopped working outside of the house. My real work comes from in the home. Raising a family. Tending to the horses. Keeping Frank happy. And I'm real happy, baby. I wouldn't trade my life for anything. Not one thing. You think about that. I've grown up in foster care and been with families who only wanted me for the check the state gave 'em each month to keep me alive. I didn't have the best of upbringings. You would have thought a person like me would have steered clear of having babies."

Just like me, thought Fiona. Although not raised in foster care, she didn't have the best of home lives. However, just because it had worked for C.C. didn't mean it could work for her. They were two different people, with two different lives.

"I've seen the way you and your fiancé look at each other. That man would move heaven and earth to give you want you want. So what is it? What is it that you want, dear?"

At that moment, she didn't know. She knew she wanted nothing more than to make Ned happy. But what she wanted for herself was a different story. Her throat closed tight and her eyes watered before she could stop her body's reaction to the intense question. What was she doing? Why was she getting so upset? Because she knew she was about to turn her back on the best man, the best friend, she'd ever had and it was all her fault.

"Excuse me. I need to go to your bathroom." Fiona rushed down the hall to one of the many bathrooms. She barely had the door closed before she leaned over the toilet and purged her guts out.

What a way to start a Fourth of July barbeque.

\* ~ \*

Ned turned to the back door of the house for a fifth time while Chunti was talking to see if Fiona was on her way out. Standing with Chunti annoyed the hell out of him and he missed Fiona.

"She's only been gone for fifteen minutes, son." Fat Bastard slapped Ned on his arm to get his attention. "You're away from her more than eight hours a day, five days a week. I'm sure you can stand another five or so minutes, can't you?"

Ned feigned a smile as he rubbed the sore spot on his arm. The man hit like a linebacker. It was okay though. Ned needed the abuse. Since he knew Fiona wouldn't knock any sense into him, someone had to abuse him.

"Anyway, this is Max Hedrow. Need I say more?" Chunti smirked but the name was enough.

Ned eagerly shook the man's hand. "It's a pleasure to meet you, Mr. Hedrow." Had he known the CEO of the company was going to be at Fat Bastard's party, he would have worn a better shirt. "My name is Ned Cholurski. I work in your programming department."

"And do you enjoy it there?" Hedrow asked.

Ned cut his eyes over to Chunti. What the hell was he supposed to say? No. It sucks big, hairy donkey balls to work for a man who never remembered his name, only invited him to his party to ogle his pretend fiancée and was a drunk, homophobe and a host of other things that probably shouldn't be said in mixed company? Or maybe he should do what Fiona would want him to do, which was be kind, courteous, and appreciative. Overall, lie.

No. He'd done enough of that these last few days. He was over playing a puppet. He didn't have to be brutal but he would be honest.

"I think my talents could be best used elsewhere," Ned said with his shoulders back, his chest out and his voice booming.

Chunti's smile twitched but he covered it with a drink and a nervous laugh, in that order. "Yeah, I told you he had some idea about taking my job. Look at the balls on this kid." He let out a heartier laugh.

"Not take your job, sir. I have ideas that could significantly boost Meta Corporation's image and stock earnings." Ned spoke slowly, clearly, and distinctly so that none of his words could be misunderstood.

"Now you're talking my language." Hedrow pointed to him with his middle finger as he held onto his drink. At least it looked like the man was drinking iced tea, unlike Chunti, who must have been on his third bourbon. Who knew what the man had had before Ned got there.

"Come on, guys. Let's not talk business now. This is a party." Chunti raised his arms in the air and laughed as though the rest of the guests would join him in his private merriment.

When a waiter walked by with a tray of food, Chunti prompted him to shove the tray at Hedrow and Ned. After surveying the lot, Ned settled on something like looked like potted meat on a cracker. Had there been fruit or vegetables on the tray, he would have gone for that. But this was the safest option he found.

"Chunti tells me you have some great ideas." Hedrow took a bite of the thing that looked like a fish eyeball on a Ritz cracker.

"Yes, I have an idea dealing with cell phones, e-mail and a paging system that..."

Hedrow cut him off. "Oh, I know that. Chunti told me about that idea."

Ned lifted his eyebrows in surprise. So Fat Bastard did talk him up to the boss. Maybe he wasn't such a bastard after all. Now he would have to think of another nickname to call him. Big Man. No. Large And In Charge. Nope, too long.

Ned took a bite of his crap on a cracker as soon as Hedrow said, "So are you working on that project with Chunti since it was his idea or did you have some other one in mind?"

Ned didn't mean to spit the tasteless crap all over Hedrow's face, but the statement and the horrible food caught him off guard.

*Chunti's idea?* Fiona had warned him but Ned had felt safe just giving him a brief overview. But instead he'd stabbed Ned in the back.

Wiping off his face, Hedrow said, "I know the food's not that great, Ned, but you don't have to..."

"*His* idea? Chunti said that was his idea?" Ned pointed to the now red-faced Fat Bastard who now deserved a fitting last name. Fat Bastard Toad Shit.

"I think the boy's had too much to drink." Chunti took Hedrow's glass and pointed him to the pool house where he could get cleaned up. Alone, he pulled Ned away from any prying ears. "Look, Ned."

Must have been serious. It was the first time in three years that the man remembered his real name.

"I'm hanging on by a string here at Meta. I know it was wrong to take credit for your idea but I've got nothing."

Yeah, nothing but a huge house, a pool, millions in the bank and a wife who adores him for some ungodly reason.

He said with his voice low, "Tell me your full plan. Tell me your idea about this cell phone, e-mail, pager thingy and I'll make sure to give you whatever you want. A raise."

A raise would be nice. But damn, he needed more than that. Fiona had made him realize what an asset Ned really was to the Meta Corporation. And now Chunti confirmed that fact. If he wanted, he had a lot of leverage.

Chunti must have noticed Ned's hesitation because he quickly followed with, "Your own office with a view."

That offer was a little better. But giving up his idea didn't sit right with him. Besides, if Ned could get a job at Meta, he could get a job anywhere. He shook his head and started to walk away when Chunti hit him with an offer he couldn't refuse.

"Your fiancée. She wanted to meet Judge Kristoff. He's here. I can guarantee to make her a clerk in his courtroom if you help me."

* ~ *

Fiona had finally made it outside to the party. This wasn't a typical barbeque with a grill going and beach balls and a volleyball net. No, this was definitely a corporate barbeque, including catering and a swing band. Guess they thought that was hip.

She grabbed a ginger ale from a passing waitress to settle her stomach and picked up what looked to be chopped liver on a cracker. Couldn't be too bad. She took a bite.

Her eyes watered immediately and she had to spit the offending food into a nearby bush. She hoped no one saw her but even if they did, she would have had to tell them that food was an abomination to dog crap.

Turning back to the house, Fiona entered through the back door and made her way into the kitchen where the wait staff bustled around. She tried staying out of their way as she surveyed the catered food. Oysters on the half shell, sitting out on the counter without any ice or refrigeration, overcooked tuna, a soggy cake. Who the hell came up with this mess?

Fiona looked into the refrigerator to see if she could come up with a meal to salvage the oysters before they went out to the unsuspecting guests.

Her eyes widened at the array of food she found and she quickly came up with an idea for a dish that was easy to make and quick. Plus it helped that it was her favorite. As the ideas rolled in her head over what she would make, her heart pounded. Her skin tingled. It was like sex but better.

A server came into the kitchen looking for another tray to take out.

"Pots and pans. Do you know where I can find them?" Fiona asked her.

She shook her head. "I'm a temp with the wait staff. I would think either down there or up in those cabinets. I'm not sure." She grabbed a tray of hors d'oeuvres and exited as fast as she came in.

"Looking for this?"

The deep voice that came from behind her made her jump and put a hand to her chest. In contrast to the hustle and bustle of the party, she found the kitchen to be very quiet and didn't expect that someone else could be in there with her.

Behind her stood a man, a very distinguished man, with gray hair, silvery blue eyes, a natural-looking tan and a slight smile with a skillet in his hand. His bright, crisp white shirt was unbuttoned at the top and his tan khakis looked starched within an inch of its life. She would bet her life savings that he wasn't wearing socks in his boat shoes.

"Thank you." She accepted the pan and put it to the stove. After turning on the stove eye she looked around for something to put over her clothes. Noticing her frantic search, the man handed her an apron.

"I recognize the look of someone who knows their way around the kitchen but doesn't want to get too messy. Been there myself." He smiled wider.

It made her want to smile with him. "So you cook too?"

"Trying to learn. I take lessons. Takes my mind off of work." He sat on the other side of the island as he watched Fiona work her magic. "What about you?"

"Home taught and self-taught. I love to cook. Actually my real dream is to go to culinary school and become a chef."

She blinked at the admission. It was the first time she'd admitted out loud to anyone, even herself, that her dream was to be a chef. But she couldn't deny her passion. She loved to cook. It relaxed her. Nothing bad ever happened in her kitchen. She felt it was much more exciting than the law.

"So what are you planning on doing now?" he asked.

She looked at him and smiled. "I can save this party or I can save us. Which should I do?"

He laughed. "These people are friends of mine. I don't know about your cooking skills. Show me what you can do and then we'll decide about the party."

"Deal."

Taking about four of the oysters, Fiona whipped up a dish that smelled wonderful. Scents of olive oil and sweet basil filled this dream of a kitchen. It was a huge, airy room with caramel colored hardwood floors so glossy it looked like there was a clear donut glaze coating it. She admired the Sub-Zero refrigerator big enough to hide a body. The Viking stove that brought a tear to her eye whenever she touched a knob. And more cabinets than she'd ever seen in her life. Gadgets lined the counters. Blenders, Cuisinarts, mixers of all types, espresso machines, coffee grinders. Whatever she wanted, they had it and then some.

Once she was done with the dish, she handed a plate of it to the mysterious man who stayed out of her way when she cooked but offered to help when she needed a certain ingredient or appliance. The man looked at her warily, stabbed the tines of his fork into a succulent oyster that made Fiona want to sample it, and he popped it in his mouth.

She waited for his expression. That was the true reward for a chef. How would people react? The man rolled his eyes to the back of his head before closing his eyes and relaxing his shoulders.

"Delicious!" he exclaimed. "How did you do that in such a short time?"

"You watched me. I have no secrets." Her heart throbbed at the idea that someone other than her family and Ned had enjoyed her cooking. If only she could do that on a bigger scale. Have her own restaurant maybe or even own her own catering service. She would do a much better job than the clown running *this* service.

"This is wonderful." The man continued downing the dish as he alternated between eating and drinking his white wine. "May I at least get the name of the angel of mercy who saved me from a fate worse than death?"

After wiping her hands on her apron, she came around the stove island and extended her hand. "Fiona Griffen. I'm the fian..." She nearly continued the lie that had gotten her here, but she couldn't do that anymore. "I'm a friend of one of the guests here," she amended.

"Well, friend of a guest, I think you definitely have a great start in the culinary business. By the way, my name is Cass."

She sat down next to him and let out a long sigh.

"That didn't sound good." He finished off his wine and poured more into his glass. He offered her some but she declined, not being in the mood to drink. Her mind had been on too many things, including Ned and what the hell she was doing here.

"It's not good. But you don't have time to hear about my woes. Besides, this is a party. Shouldn't we be having fun?" She tried plastering a fake smile on her face.

"Who are you kidding?" He gently chuckled.

Guess she'd lost that cheerleader spirit.

"These parties are nothing but reasons to press the flesh, and I mean that business-wise and otherwise, if you get my drift." He flitted his eyebrows and Fiona got his meaning.

Was there a predator around every corner or did Chunti just attract all of them to his house? She'd never thought *this* guy could be on the make. He seemed so nice to her, so kind. She stood and took off her apron.

"Glad you liked the dish. I should be getting out to the party."

"Oh please, honey, I wasn't coming on to you." He waved her back to her seat. "Come on. Let's talk. You're about the only interesting person here and I'm including my dear friends, the Chuntis."

Taking tentative steps back to the barstool next to the man, Fiona sat back down and kept her legs crossed. Now she was glad she'd worn pants and a mock turtleneck top.

"So tell me your troubles. I hear enough of them during the week. It would be nice to hear someone tell the truth for a change." He chuckled and took another sip of his wine.

She didn't know if it was his honest eyes or the warmth of his voice, but Fiona decided to take a chance. She blurted out the plan with Ned, but left out the steamy sex. She didn't know Cass that well. When she got to the part about Judge Kristoff, his eyes seemed to light up. If Cass knew Chunti, then he probably knew Kristoff too.

So she was sabotaging her chances of ever working for the man and getting into law. Although she had planned to throw obstacles in her way that would keep her from getting the job, telling the whole truth did feel wonderful.

"That's a heck of a story," Cass said and finished off his second glass of wine.

"Sounds unbelievable." She rubbed her eyes and wondered how long she and Ned would have to stay at this party before they could make a quick exit.

"Sounds like you're in love with this Ned guy."

She blinked at Cass' assessment of her feelings.

"Are you? Are you in love with him?" he asked again.

Fiona didn't have to think long on the answer. She nodded. "But I'm just afraid that he'll reject me because I lied. I wanted to be serious and have a serious career and, yes, I got really great grades. But why would he want a former cheerleader who wants to cook for a living? He's a really smart man. He deserves to be with a really intelligent, professional woman who knows what she wants in life."

"Sounds like he's got it." He put his hand on hers and the gesture felt genuine, not a come on. "You. It takes a smart woman to know what she wants, to know what's best for people. And if the law is not what you really want to do, then don't do it. For God's sake, don't be one of those miserable people who work in a profession they hate. If you're going to do something, do something you love. You'll be happy and you'll make him happy."

She didn't know if it was because of his sound advice or because he offered his help when he didn't need to, but Fiona wrapped her arms around the man's neck and hugged him.

"Thank you. That was the best thing anyone has done for me," she said.

"It's what I do best, assess the situation and render a solution." He patted her on the back in a comforting manner.

She righted herself on her stool and picked up Cass' plate to dish him out more food. The man certainly deserved it.

"So you never told me what it is that you do. You said you listen to lies all week. With your sound advice, I would think you're a psychiatrist." She spooned out more of the oyster dish she'd made.

Cass laughed. "Close enough. I'm a criminal court judge."

Fiona froze.

"I'm Judge Casper Kristoff."

Her hand shook and she dropped the plate onto the floor.

# *Chapter 14*

## *Never accept the first offer*

Where the hell was Fiona when Ned needed her? Here Chunti had laid this big offer that could help him out a little but help Fiona out a lot, and he wanted her advice, her input. He had to face it. Over the years, she'd proved herself really smart when it came to business matters and common sense things.

Hell, what was he doing? He didn't need a committee vote. He just had to listen to his heart. His heart told him that he should do what was right for Fiona. He would give anything to make her happy. And if what made her happy was working for this Kristoff guy, then he would make a deal with the devil.

"So what's it going to be?" Chunti asked. His face glowed with sweat and from the intense heat. The sun baked him until he looked like he would pop.

"Can I think about it?" Ned asked, wanting to stall for time.

"Son, the party is here and now. Fiona's here. Kristoff's here. I'm not going to arrange something later on. Tell me now. Do we have a deal? Your own office, a raise."

"And a title change," Ned countered.

Chunti squirmed. His face squished around like a kaleidoscope. "If I do that, then Hedrow will suspect you had something to do with the project. I'll just say you're working on a special project and that's why you have the new office."

"Which means when this imaginary special project is over, you can boot me back to my old cubicle, right?" Ned *would* be selling his soul to the devil if he agreed to these shoddy terms. He would be working twice as hard with a tiny raise and no title change, plus Chunti would have his idea and get the credit.

"Come on, son. Stop thinking about yourself and think about your woman. What do you think she would want?"

The question stopped him cold. It was one of the reasons he wanted to talk to her first. He had a feeling she wanted to reveal something to him but never got the chance before the Chunti ambush.

Then he remembered her packed bags next to her bed before they left for the party. If she were going to leave him, then he wanted to be sure to do something special for her, something for which she would remember him for the rest of her life, wherever she may be.

"Fine. I'll do it," Ned said, conceding. His heartbeat slowed until it felt like it pumped once a minute. Fiona would probably hate that he gave up his idea to Chunti. But he would only do something like this for her. Only her.

"Wise decision. Come into the house and we'll talk about the idea and your terms." Chunti put his hand on Ned's shoulder and it felt like a searing heat cut through his shirt to burn his flesh.

Why did doing the right thing feel so wrong?

* ~ *

"Oh my God! I'm so sorry!" Fiona crouched to the floor and scooped up the broken pieces of what had to be an expensive plate from a very old set of china.

Kristoff seemed to be laughing at her as he helped her clean up the mess. "Why are you apologizing, dear?"

"For telling you what a horrible person I am. For breaking this plate I know I'll never be able to pay for no matter how long I work. For treating you like the help. I feel like such an idiot." Her frantic rantings didn't stop Kristoff from depositing the broken pieces into a trash can and wiping up the rest of the food with a paper towel.

"For one thing, I'll take the blame for the plate. Lord knows Frank owes me enough favors for all the things I've gotten him out of over the last few years. Point two, you never treated me like the help. I wanted to help you cook. And point three, I don't think you're a horrible person."

He stood and helped her to her feet. She was sure her eyes were red from tears as she tried desperately to keep her gaze from him. "You don't?"

"No. I've had people do worse things than you to get into my courtroom." He wiped her eyes with a handkerchief he pulled from his pocket. "I thought your name sounded familiar. You called my courtroom on several occasions. Bad part about it is that you would have been great in my courtroom. You're conscientious and thorough and honest. I need a person like that."

She smiled.

"But you're right. I wouldn't have hired you."

She frowned.

"Not for my courtroom."

She furrowed her eyebrows. "What do you mean?"

"I want you in another position."

The statement sounded lascivious. She took a step back and put her hand on the counter near the pan. If needed, she could grab the handle and whack this joker in the head.

"You're getting that look again in your eyes." He stepped up closer to her and whispered, "Look, you shared something personal with me so I'll share something with you. I'm gay."

Fiona tried to keep the stunned expression from her face but the way Kristoff chuckled, she guessed she wasn't doing a very good job.

"Frank doesn't know but C.C. does. I think she likes that Frank has one gay friend because he can be such a son of a bitch."

His honesty made her laugh. "I didn't know."

"No one really knows. I keep my personal life out of the papers because I hope one day to get into politics. But voters still don't look kindly to gay politicians so I'm keeping a low profile."

"If it's any consolation, I would vote for you."

He patted her hand. "Means a lot, dear." He led her back to her chair and handed her a glass of water.

Guess her trembling hands and the newly formed sweat on her forehead gave her nervousness away. All this time, all this scheming, just so she could meet Judge Kristoff. She finally met the man and she'd admitted what a dishonest person she was in trying to meet him.

"So if I can't work for you in your courtroom what did you mean you still wanted me?" she asked.

"Cooking. I told you I'm a horrible cook. I'm taking lessons but I have no time to devote to doing it properly. I have a woman now who cleans for me and sometimes prepares a meal or two but it's nothing grand. What I want is a chef who can think on her feet."

Fiona shook her head. "I don't want to come off as a snob, Judge Kristoff..."

"Cass," he said, cutting her off. "You knew me as Cass way before you knew I was a judge."

"Okay, Cass, I'm not a snob but I don't want to be your maid."

This time he blinked. "I don't want you to be my maid. I'll pay for you to go to culinary school here. I believe there's a Johnson and Wales school locally. You'll come over to my home two or three times a week and teach me to cook. Maybe once a month I'll throw a dinner party that you'll cater. If all goes well, if you want to have a catering business, I'll be more than happy to help get you on the road to starting it or turn you on to some people who can help you."

This time the tears that streamed down her cheeks were from happiness. She hugged him so hard she thought she would break his neck but she couldn't let him go.

"Thank you," she said between tears. "You don't know what this means to me."

"Oh, I think I do. Besides, anyone who can work miracles in this kitchen deserves every break she can get."

She laughed with him and only stopped when she heard a voice behind her.

"What's going on here?" C.C. strolled up to the duo. "Looks like the party is in here."

Fiona broke from the embrace and wiped her eyes. "Judge-- uh, I mean Cass, has just made me a terrific offer. I'm going to be a chef."

C.C. held Fiona's hand. Must be a thing in the Chunti house. Before a person can express a thought or idea she had to hold a hand.

"Is this what you really want?" C.C. asked.

Fiona nodded so hard her neck ached. "It's always been my dream." She glanced at Kristoff. "Well, part of a dream." She got her wish to work for Kristoff, just not in the way she thought she would.

C.C. put her pug nose in the air and took in a big whiff. "What smells so good? I know it's not from the catering service."

"No. That's from our little chef here. She whipped up a dish using those oysters in a matter of minutes. It was simply divine." Kristoff kissed this side of her face like a proud father.

The gesture brought another wave of tears to her eyes.

When C.C. walked by her trash can she noticed her broken plate. "What is that?"

Fiona gasped and Kristoff covered it by talking over her. "I dropped it."

The old Fiona would have let that story go. But not the new Fiona. "No, he didn't, C.C. *I* dropped it. He's covering for me because I know it must be an expensive plate and I couldn't possibly afford to replace it. I'm so sorry. I'll do whatever I can to make up for it."

"It's okay, dear. Belonged on Frank's side of the family. Can't stand his family anyway." She laughed and sat on one of the barstools. "If you make me what you made Cass, I'll call it even."

"Deal." Fiona broke from Cass' embrace and started on a second dish for C.C.

"Besides," C.C. began as Kristoff made his way next to her, "I was all thumbs too when I was in your condition."

"What condition is that?" Fiona asked ask she heated up the stove and grabbed a plateful of oysters.

"Pregnant."

A second plate crashed to the floor.

* ~ *

As Chunti led Ned from the house, a partygoer grabbed Chunti's arm.

"Time for a speech, Frank," the man said.

"Fine. Fine." Chunti turned to Ned. "We'll discuss the finer details after I speak. You've done a good thing here, son."

Folding the paper with Ned's idea into a small square, Chunti shoved the wad into his front shorts pocket. He winked and teetered off.

Ned nodded, feeling numb to what he'd just done. He felt like a father giving up his newborn child. But his heart was in the right place. He'd given his idea to Chunti for Fiona. He would have given more for her if needed. With that thought, he took a deep breath and blew out a ragged exhalation.

His gaze took in the expansive property. The lush green lawn against the very blue swimming pool made the area look like it came out of a cartoon or painting. Matched with the light blue sky and the dark green leaves on the tree, the rich colors seemed too much. Maybe it wasn't the colors so much as the situation.

Ned had to sit down on a bench and take deep breaths as he thought about the offer. For some reason Steve Jobs and Bill Gates skipped through his mind. Bad deals. Bad deals. Only those guys did it for greed. He did this for love.

Fiona. The woman of his dreams and his best friend. She would understand why he'd done it. It was for her, all for her.

When he directed his attention toward Chunti on the stage where the band played, he continued taking in deep breaths to calm himself down. The sweat that had formed on his forehead cooled him when the breeze kicked up. It was only when he saw the catering van pull up to the side of the house and the driver of the van coming out of it that he became overheated again.

Kwame. He'd almost forgotten that that bastard owned a catering company. Who knew Chunti would have hired this joker to work his party? When he saw him going into the house, Ned's heart started pounding.

Fiona. She was still in there. If she saw him, she would get upset. He would bother her like last time. This time he was ready for him. Ned bolted up from the bench and stormed over to the back door.

"This has been a great year for Meta Corporation," Chunti said before Ned ducked into the house. "I see us breaking our way through another realm of business and kicking butt there too!"

The crowd applauded as soon as Ned disappeared into the house.

* ~ *

"Now one plate I can explain off to Frank, but not two," C.C. said as she helped Fiona clean up the mess.

"You just caught me off guard with what you said." Fiona let the word tumble in her head. Pregnant. Pregnant. Baby. Baby. Baby. "I think you're mistaken."

"After seven of my own and twenty grandbabies, I know the signs."

Logically, Fiona knew the woman was wrong. She and Ned had only been having sex that week. No way in the world could she know this soon. And she had been a faithful pill-taker since the age of seventeen. She never missed a dose.

But what if she *was* pregnant? She'd always said she never wanted a child, but thinking about carrying Ned's child warmed her heart. Without really thinking, she put her hand to her stomach.

She shook her head. "No, C.C., I can't be pregnant. I..."

"Pregnant? Who's the daddy?"

Fiona directed her attention to the back door and was stunned to see Kwame. She shouldn't have been. From the poor food quality, lazy wait staff and lousy food selection, she should have guessed it was Kwame's catering company.

Knowing what he did for a living was the main reason she had been attracted to him. He worked in the food business so she would pick his brain on every date about how the industry worked. It made him attractive until she went on a job with him and saw how bad he was at the catering business.

"Who are you?" Cass asked, indignation lacing his voice.

"I'm the caterer. I'm also her man." He pointed to Fiona.

She shook her head. "No, you're not. We used to go out and now we don't. Get over it, Kwame."

"Yeah, I see you've gotten over it with some other punk, huh? He got you knocked up?" Kwame rubbed his hand on Fiona's stomach. His rough touch made her want to throw up again. Instead she jumped back and kept her gaze down to the floor.

"Young man, we pay you for food services, not to accost the guests. I suggest you either serve or get out without pay." C.C. stood between him and Fiona like a guard dog. Fiona barely knew C.C., but she loved the woman already.

"And trust me, as a judge, I'll make sure that if she doesn't pay for services that any lawsuit you file will not make it to court for several years." Cass stood next to C.C. to make a human shield in front of her. "And then there's the valid assault charge when you put your hands on this young lady without her permission."

"And if you lay a hand on her again, I'll break every bone in your body."

Kwame turned around and laughed hysterically when he saw Ned. Fiona's stomach fluttered. She was both happy to see him and scared. The last time he faced Kwame, the results weren't stellar.

"White boy coming to the rescue again?" Kwame said when he gained composure. "Punk, you remember the last time you tried to square off. Don't make me have to whup your ass again."

"You watch your language in my house and in front of my guests," C.C. said, this time picking up a rolling pin. This woman meant business.

"Fine. Whatever. I came to get my check and go anyway."

"Not until you apologize to Mrs. Chunti, Fiona and this gentleman here," Ned said, his jaw set in.

"Ned, just let it go. Let him go." Fiona didn't want to sound like she was pleading but she didn't want to see anyone get hurt, especially Ned. She loved him.

"Yeah, listen to your, um, roommate. Or are you the baby's daddy?"

Ned had a look of confusion covering his face as he looked at Fiona. *Baby?* What was this asshole talking about?

"Just get out of here," Ned said, deciding he would get to the bottom of that statement after Kwame left.

Kwame gazed back at the trio. Looking at C.C. he said, "Mail me my check." Turning to Kristoff he spat, "Fag!" Then peering over their shoulders to Fiona he said, "Bitch. You ain't worth my time anyway. You talk too damn much for a hot chick anyway."

He attempted to push his way past Ned but Ned had heard enough. No way would he let him insult Fiona and these other nice people who had protected her. He'd had his fill of bullies. He wouldn't let himself or anyone else get belittled or pushed around if he could help it.

This time Kwame made the first move and gave Ned a hard shove back.

"Ned!" Fiona screamed as she tried to get past C.C. The woman held her around her waist and wouldn't let her go.

* ~ *

"I'm calling the police." The other man in front of Fiona said as he darted to a phone.

Ned grabbed Kwame by his collar and shoved him against the wall, rolling from one wall to another until they broke through the back screen door and onto the lawn. He heard the collective group gasps from the guests as they stood far enough back from the tussling duo but close enough to get a good look.

"I don't mind kicking your ass in front of all of these people," Kwame said as they rolled on the grass.

"Neither do I," Ned replied, hatred and rage feeding his strength.

He had Kwame on his back and with a quick jab of a raised knee, he got him square between his legs. As Kwame doubled over in pain, his hands going to his crotch, Ned rolled him back onto his back, raised his fist into the air and was about to give him the punch he so wanted to lay into him that night at the club.

"Ned!"

Fiona's voice broke his thoughts as he looked over at her. She got free from C.C.'s grip and made it to them.

"This isn't you. You're not a violent animal like this scum." She framed his face with her delicate hands even as he sat on top of Kwame. "I know you're a good man. I know you can protect me if you had to. I don't need to see you beating Kwame to a pulp to prove anything to me or to anyone else. I love you, Ned. I love you so much."

With that, Ned sprang off of Kwame, enveloped Fiona into his arms and swung her around. "I love you too. I love you, Fi."

He set her down and kissed her passionately. His tongue slid into her hot mouth. Even with the audible gasps from the partygoers, Ned still felt like it was only the two of them standing on that lawn kissing.

Fiona broke from him and smiled. "Wait. There is something I have to do." She pulled from his embrace, walked over to Kwame and with a smile gave him a swift kick in his stomach. "Asshole. That's for punching my man."

"Wow, maybe I should have brought her in for the other position," the man who had stood in front of Fiona said.

Ned turned to him. "And you are?"

"Oh, sorry. With all that confusion in there we weren't properly introduced. I'm Casper Kristoff. I take it you're Ned the Great."

Ned shook his hand. This was the man. The one Fiona wanted to work for. Apparently if he was willing to put his body between her and Kwame she must have made one hell of an impression.

"Ned is fine," Ned said, commenting on the Ned the Great moniker.

Fiona skipped up to the two of them, radiating. "That felt too good. I see why you wanted to keep going." She kissed Ned on his cheek. "I see you've met Cass."

*Cass?* She was on a first name basis with him too?

"Yes, Judge Kristoff. I guess you two have talked?" Ned asked, gazing back and forth between the two.

"Oh yes." She smiled even wider. "I'm going to be working for him."

Ned kissed her again and swung her around even more. "That's great! It's what you've always wanted."

"Well, not exactly."

Ned set her down. "What do you mean?"

"I've always wanted to be a chef. I've never wanted to go into law. I explained all that to Cass and he's agreed to send me to culinary school and have me give him lessons three times a week and cater a dinner party once a month. Isn't that great?"

But Ned didn't share in her happiness. The smile drooped down, dragging his face with it in the fall. He stepped back. "You don't want to be a lawyer?"

Her smile slowly faded as the police sirens came closer to the house. The loud whirring noise echoed in his head.

"I never really loved the law. I tried to. I really did. But my heart has always been into cooking. You know how much I love to cook. So now I'll be doing what I love. Isn't that great?"

Ned shook his head. "You used me. This whole plan. You made a fool out of me."

"I didn't mean to. It didn't start off that way." She reached for him but he flinched back.

"Maybe you two need to talk alone," Cass said as he nodded toward the crowd that suddenly directed their attention to them instead of Kwame getting hauled away in handcuffs.

"No. Maybe I just need some time alone." He handed her the car keys as he walked past her. "I would have done anything for you. I did do the unthinkable for you. And you treated me like the other kids did in high school. Used me for what I could do for you and laugh about it afterward. I thought I knew you."

He walked away from her, from the situation. He was tired of making a fool of himself. He was tired of being made a fool of. And she said she loved him. What a joke. She loved him for what he could do for her. Nothing more.

So why was he hurting so much?

\* ~ \*

170

Fiona's heart crashed against her rib cage and slid down the inside of her body. She could feel it. She'd crushed him the way she never wanted to.

"I can't believe this," was all Fiona could say as she watched Ned walk away from her, walk out of her life. "This can't be happening. I can't lose him."

Cass put his arms around her and held her as she wept. He leaned down and whispered, "You want me to have him arrested?"

She knew he meant it as a joke but she cried even harder.

"Kidding, dear. Only kidding."

But she wasn't. The best thing that ever happened to her just walked out of her life. What the hell was she supposed to do now?

# *Chapter 15*

### *Sometimes it's okay to start from square one*

"More cookies, dear?" Ned's mom asked him, breaking his thoughts.

He'd been staring at the TV screen for God knows how long, looking at the Weather Channel, but not really taking in what was going on. His mind remained on Fiona. How could she have used him? 'We'll play like we're a couple,' she'd said. 'No one will get hurt,' she said. 'I love you.' That was the one that really hurt.

"No, I'm fine, Mom. Thanks." Ned picked up the remote and turned it to another channel, something to keep his mind off of Fiona. He settled on a channel that was playing the second Matrix movie. Rebirth. Revolutions. One of those. This had enough noise in it to keep his mind occupied. Then the character Jada Pinkett Smith played appeared on the screen.

Ned sat up and took notice. He couldn't deny how much Fiona looked like her except Fiona was taller and way sexier. He had heard Jada was about five feet tall, maybe an inch or two above that but not much more. And he missed Fiona. His body ached for her like she was a drug.

But he would have to wean himself off of her. She'd lied. She'd hurt him. He was still smarting over it. What he didn't understand was that if she really didn't want to be in law, why couldn't she tell him that? Why the elaborate scheme? Did she really love him and want to be with him but didn't know how to go about telling him? Did she really think he would turn her down?

Hell, they'd been best friends.

He stretched his long legs out on the coffee table as he sat in his parents' rec room. It was the same room he and Fiona used to study in when they were in high school.

The walls were still covered in paneling but at least his parents replaced the shag carpeting with a more contemporary oatmeal-colored Berber carpet. And the furniture had all been replaced. No more green and orange. The couch and chairs were all a deep burgundy.

His mother, not one to remain quiet when she had an opinion, sat in a chair opposite him. "On vacation from work?" she asked.

"Quit."

After he realized that he would go nowhere while working at Meta Corporation, Ned returned to work Monday only to clean out his desk, retrieve all of his files and turn in his badge. He'd given up his great idea to Chunti. Now he would have to start all over at another business, another job he would hate. Another group of people to rename. Who needed the headache? He would take some time off and find out what it was that he wanted.

"Oh, I was wondering why you've been here for over a week," his mom said, cutting into his rambling thoughts.

"Needed some time to myself." He clicked the remote to a station that played nothing but cartoons. Nothing on *there* that would remind him of Fiona.

His mother reached down to the coffee table and picked up the red ring box. She didn't open it. "And Fiona?"

He shifted his weight on the couch to get comfortable but never answered her question.

"Ned?"

"I don't know. We haven't spoken since I've been here."

That day after the barbeque, he'd walked all the way home. Once he'd gotten there, she was waiting for him. She'd wanted to talk. He'd wanted more time. So he'd packed a bag and left without a word.

"Does she know you're here?"

Deciding to keep his mouth full to prevent from answering any more questions, he bent over to the coffee table and shoved a chocolate chip cookie into it. It was good. But he had to admit, Fiona's cookies were better. Crunchy around the edges, soft in the middle. Just a hint of butter and the right amount of nutmeg. He licked his tongue around his lips to retrieve the excess crumbs.

"I asked you a question, son."

"No, ma'am. I doubt if she knows I'm here." He kept his gaze from his mother, knowing the disappointed look she would give him.

"Don't you think you should call her? Invite her over for dinner? Talk to her? She's your best friend."

"Don't want to talk about her right now."

His mother stood. Before she left the room, she said, "I just know good friends are hard to come by." She kissed his forehead. "And you'll never find another love of your life again."

Love. What did his mother know about how he felt about
Fiona? He may have loved her at one time. But not now. Not
when their last week had been nothing but a lie.

"Your father and I are going to your uncle's for bridge
night. Want to join us?"

Ned shook his head, keeping his gaze on the TV.

"If you change your mind..."

"I know."

"Dinner's in the oven. You know the phone number to your
uncle's if you need us?"

"Mom, I'm not a kid anymore. I can take care of myself."
He didn't mean to snap at his mother, but she was being a bit
smothering right now.

"Oh, funny. You're acting like a child so I thought I'd treat
you like one."

"You just don't get it," he said, finally facing her. "She lied
to me. Used to be when people treated me badly you would
stick up for me. But I guess things have changed, huh?"

His mother stopped at the top step. Her black, curly hair
peppered with gray wiggled when she whipped her head
around, returning her gaze to him. She put her hand on her
ample hip but it was hard for her to look intimidating when the
woman wore sky blue polyester shorts, a red checkered
sleeveless shirt and black socks with her white Naturalizer
sneakers. But she was an angry mom nonetheless and
commanded his attention.

"You are exactly like your father," she began. "He was
clueless when it came to women too."

"Clueless?"

"Yes. That woman loves you whether you think so or not.
She has ever since she skipped home with you with those little
pigtails in her hair. And do you know how I could tell?"

He really didn't want her gloating more but he couldn't deny he was more than curious to know how his mother figured out Fiona loved him before he could guess.

"Because she would come over here under the guise of getting help with her French homework and the child spoke it and knew it like a natural. I sat outside the door and listened to the two of you. You would say a sentence and she would correct your mistakes. She would blow through all of her sentences and say them perfectly. And you know what? Half of the time she was saying in French how cute she thought you were and how she was glad you two were friends, and you thought she was saying that 'Claude had a cow in his yard' or whatever sentence she was supposed to translate."

Ned opened his mouth to refute her statement. Surely he hadn't been sitting with Fiona while she said in French she thought he was cute and he never picked up on it. Now that he thought about it, he'd never really listened to what Fiona had said when she spoke. He'd been too enamored with the fact that she was sitting in his house, eating his food, drinking his milk, and helping him instead of making fun of him. He'd watched her mouth move as she spoke each word and imagined he would be able to one day kiss those lips.

"You're wrong, Mom," Ned said, then shoved another cookie into his mouth. That would be his new plan. Forget about dating again. He would just stay in his parents' recreation room and eat all of their food until he became huge. It could work.

"Ned, honey, did you forget that your father and I spent our summers in France as exchange students? That was the whole reason you decided to take French instead of Spanish because you wanted my help. I understood her perfectly. I guess you never told her that you had parents who knew French. But I guess that's not a lie in your book, right?"

He didn't dare look at his mother now ... especially when she was right. He had left out the fact that his parents regularly spoke French around the house from Fiona. He'd hoped that in all of the trips to the house that they wouldn't talk that way while she was there and give away the fact that if he truly needed help that he could go to his mom or dad. But his omission was completely different from her lie. He hadn't used her.

No, but he used his ignorance to get her to come home with him.

Mothers. They knew everything.

"And since you can't love anyone who lies to you, let me tell you all the little secrets we've been keeping from you," she began. "Your Uncle Ivan played Santa every year during Christmas. Your father and I bought your presents. I know you thought Nintendo came from the North Pole but it didn't."

"Okay, Mom, I get it." He held up his hand to stop her.

"But wait. There's more. After you and I colored Easter eggs when you were a kid, your father and I hid them the night before. I put money under your pillow and took your tooth instead of the Tooth Fairy. My kisses never really healed your wounds; the Neosporin did. In the nursery rhyme 'Hey, Diddle, Diddle,' cows can't jump over the moon, and dishes and spoons can't run."

"Now you're just being ridiculous." Ned set his feet on the floor and turned his full attention to her.

"I told you I didn't have any more kids because you were my perfect angel and I stopped with you." His mother shook her head. "Not true. I had a horrible delivery with you. I nearly died. I had to have an emergency hysterectomy after you were born and I couldn't have any more children. So now you can be angry with me if you've always wanted a little brother or sister and never got one."

His body went cold at the admission. Neither his mother nor father had ever told him that. He'd always been told that they wanted only one child. But he felt a longing in them especially when he went to his cousins' house and his parents watched all of their kids playing with each other.

"Why didn't you tell me that?" he asked.

"Because you didn't need to feel guilty about my condition. You just needed to feel loved. So whatever Fiona did to you, did you feel loved at the time?"

Loved? That and then some. Physical love, emotional love, unconditional support. The woman put up with a night with Chunti for him.

"But why? I still don't get why she couldn't tell me what she really wanted." He scratched his head.

"Maybe she thought you would treat her like an idiot again." His mother pushed her glasses up her nose by pushing on the bar across the bridge of her nose.

"I've never done that!" he snapped.

"Honey, I just told you she could speak French better than most natives and you still talked to her like she didn't know a thing. The cute thing about her was that she let you. Instead of setting you straight at the outset, she let you take the lead. That girl could do cartwheels around you where French was concerned and I'm not saying that because she used to be a cheerleader. So maybe she did something else to impress you because she thought you wouldn't think there was much to her. For a man with a high IQ, you aren't very smart, are you?" She walked out of the room.

Ned rolled his eyes, something else his mother would have commented on had she caught it. "I'm going to run around the house with scissors in my hands!" he screamed after her.

"Great. Have a good time, dear."

His mother. A sarcastic wit as always.

Once the front door shut he turned the volume up on the TV to drown out his thoughts.

With every moment, every free second, he thought of nothing but Fiona. He could hear her plaintive cry when he'd left her standing on the lawn that day at the barbeque. He couldn't erase from his mind the way she'd said, "Will I see you again?" before he'd walked out the door. Her gaze, those big, hazel eyes, burned in his brain until he rubbed his eyes thinking he could make her disappear.

When the phone rang, Ned shouted, "Hallelujah." He needed something to get his mind off of her. He would even talk to a telemarketer if they weren't too pushy or obnoxious. He headed to the kitchen to answer the phone. Although his parents had remodeled the den they still hadn't installed a phone jack in the room.

"I'm looking for Ned Cholurski," the voice said.

Trying to recall the familiar voice, Ned hesitated before answering. "Speaking."

"Well, I guess you did keep your company records up to date." The man laughed but Ned wasn't about to join the stranger in his frivolity until he knew who he was and what he wanted. "Your emergency contact number is still good."

"Okay, so you know who I am. Who are you?" Ned asked, trying to cut out the bullshit.

The man cleared his throat. "Max Hedrow."

As though the CEO of the company he used to work for could see him, Ned stood up straighter, taller. He smoothed down his T-shirt and cinched his sweat shorts as though he had to be presentable for this phone call. Then he stopped. He didn't work for Meta Corporation anymore. Why was he still getting nervous from talking to his former CEO? He could tell the guy to eat shit and die and not blink an eye.

"Did you call me for a reason? I didn't take anything from the office that wasn't mine. I left all the CDs and papers that belonged to the company there in my drawer." Ned couldn't think of any reason why the man would be calling him.

"Thought you might be interested to know that we're in the process of working on Chunti's e-mail/cell phone idea."

The news of that felt like a punch in his stomach. Ned had a feeling he would be kicking himself for a long time for his decision to give up his idea, his baby.

"Sounds great." Ned tried to keep his voice even and unaffected but bitterness laced his words.

"Well, it would be if the idea were indeed Chunti's."

Ned blinked. "But, sir, it's..."

"I can tell he doesn't know the first thing about this program and it became painfully obvious when I had him leading up a team and he couldn't give them any sort of direction. That's why I'm calling you, Ned."

Now hearing his name said by a superior at Meta made his stomach flip.

Hedrow said, "I have a branch division of Meta called Hedrow Dynamics. Maybe you've heard of it."

Heard of it? They were only the innovators in some of the most high tech technology out there. You either had to be touched by God or find the golden ticket to work in that branch of the company. Ned had neither but he did have a strong desire.

"Yes, sir, I've heard of Hedrow Dynamics." This time Ned kept his voice controlled and calm. He would play this aloof.

"Good. I'd like you to head up a team to work on this project of yours. You'll have your own office, double your salary from before, and since you'll have the title of supervisor, you'll have a company vehicle and an expense account."

"Hmm, okay." The words sounded like he was uninterested. But as he stood in his parents' kitchen with its white tiled floor, blue Formica countertop, and a small, round wooden table surrounded with four chairs, adorned with a chicken cookie jar that crowed when opened, Ned jumped around like his feet were on fire.

"Your team will consist of about five employees. Do you think that'll be enough to work on this project with you?"

He actually had a choice? Ned was in heaven. "I think five should suffice."

"Good. We'll need you back here at Meta Monday morning to start the interview process. You'll choose from internal and external candidates. Training will start in approximately three weeks. Our training facility is in Maine. You would have to be there for at least six months to a year. Would that be a problem?"

And suddenly he thought of Fiona. Maine. She would love it. Especially now. Right by the water. Very quiet. Clean air. She couldn't really complain about anything except for the harsh winters. But he could snuggle up to her to keep her warm.

Wait. No, he couldn't. He'd walked out on her without a word. Six months away from Virginia and her? Yeah, he could do it.

"No, sir. That wouldn't be a problem." He released a long breath.

"Great." Hedrow told him some particulars about his reinstatement but it went in one ear and out the other. The only thing he caught was when Hedrow said, "Welcome back."

Ned hung up the phone and braced his hands against the wall. He'd done it. After years of being the guy no one noticed, he finally got some recognition, thanks to a lying Fat Bastard.

He screamed and pumped his fist into the air. He wanted to share his good news with someone. After picking up the receiver, he automatically dialed his home to call Fiona ... then stopped. They hadn't ironed out their problems. What would he even say to her?

Hanging the phone back on its cradle, he cursed himself. Damn, he missed his best friend.

"Why can't I have it all?" he screamed up to the ceiling as though talking directly to God.

Then the doorbell rang. Was it God coming to answer his question?

Ned poked his head around the kitchen wall to see if he could tell who was at the door. He saw the top of someone's head. If he didn't know any better, he could have sworn it looked like two pigtails on a child. Unless it was someone with a child sitting on their shoulders or a really tall Girl Scout, he didn't know what to expect on the other side.

Padding to the door on bare feet, he unlocked the deadbolt and the doorknob lock and creaked the door open. What he saw made his bottom jaw drop and his eyes nearly pop out of his head.

Fiona. Only it wasn't grown-up Fiona who lived with him at the apartment. This was a Fiona from ten years ago. Ned had to rub his eyes to make sure he was seeing what he saw.

With, indeed, her hair in pigtails--had to have been a wig--tied with white ribbons, she had on her old cheerleading outfit complete with black-and-white saddle shoes and blue-and-white pompoms.

Back in high school she'd looked cute in the outfit. Now all grown up and filled out in all the right places, she looked sexy. Her firm, rounded breasts filled out the top until they strained against the fabric. The pleated skirt flared slightly over her fuller hips and rounded ass. She looked like every man's fantasy.

"What are you doing?" he asked.

"Doing what you think I did to you, making a complete and utter fool of myself to prove to you how I feel." She put her hands to her waist in typical cheerleader stance. He remembered watching her at games and pep rallies.

"Fiona, wait..."

"Ready!" she screamed. "Okay! Everywhere I go, people want to know who I am! So I tell them! I am Fiona! The big loser Fiona! And you are Ned! Wonderful Ned! If you don't forgive me! Won't you please forgive me? I might as well be dead!" She capped off her cheer with a cartwheel he didn't think she could do anymore and a split on his front lawn that brought even more fantasies into his head.

As he approached her to bring her into the house, he noticed a small audience watching the spectacle. "Good evening, Mr. Firnstein. Lovely night for a walk, huh?" The elderly man walking his Chihuahua on a pink leash nodded but kept his gaze on them until he reached the end of the block.

Ned hooked Fiona under her arms and brought her up to her feet. "Just practicing a little cheer, Mrs. Dembeck."

The woman nodded and at least turned away as she went down the street, unlike Firnstein. That man had always been a busybody.

Ned held Fiona's hand as he brought her up to the porch but she stopped before going into the house.

"I can't go in there," she said and held her stance. "If you hate me then your parents really must not like me either."

Ned sighed and framed her face into his hands. "A few things are wrong with your theory. For one, my parents adore you. It's me they're not happy with right now. Point two, you are always invited into this house. I think even if I get cut off by my family, you'll still be able to come over here." He laughed to lighten the mood but she didn't even smile. "And lastly, I don't hate you. I could never hate you."

Fiona cried. Her legs buckled until she almost fell to the ground. With a quick catch, he swept her up into his arms and carried her into the house. He brought her down to the recreation room and set her on the couch. He returned to close and lock the front door then got her a glass of water.

Her hands trembled so much as she held the glass that he had to steady her hands by wrapping his around hers.

"Why did you do that? What were you thinking?" he asked with a soft voice. He wiped away her tears with his thumb. Her smooth skin caused blood to flow into his cock and it throbbed immediately. Man, now was not the time.

"You thought I used you like people used you in high school. I wanted to show you that no matter who you were, whether you thought you were the school geek..."

He winced at that remark but made no comment.

"--or even the head cheerleader, you were made fun of."

"What are you talking about? You were the most popular girl in school."

"Yeah, everyone loved Fiona. But no one thought I had a brain in my head. No one figured I would do anything in life but be the quarterback's wife and pop out a bunch of babies. Or maybe a flight attendant. That's why I wanted to go into a field that would prove everyone wrong. The law seemed to shut a lot of people up." She sniffed and her red-eyed gaze captured his. "And I wanted to prove to you that you didn't have to be ashamed to have me on your arm."

Ned pulled his hand back and blinked hard. "Ashamed? Me ashamed of you? Where would you get an idea like that?"

Fiona snatched a couple of sheets of facial tissue from a box next to the couch. While dabbing her eyes she said, "Smart guys don't want to be with dumb women. They want a woman they can talk to, have interesting conversations with, have common interests. I thought if I looked interesting, then you would notice me."

"Honey, I noticed you the first day I saw you. Kinda hard not to when you look like you do."

She smirked and he realized very quickly how he'd proven her point. She wanted to be recognized for what was inside instead of her beauty.

"I'm sorry," he said.

"My looks opened doors. But I want my *mind* to keep me in the room. You were the first guy, at least on the outside, who didn't seem to care that I was the head cheerleader. You never really talked down to me." She held his hands. "You know when I knew you were truly special?"

He shook his head and held his breath waiting for the answer.

"It was the day in chemistry class when we had to pair up and you chose me to be your partner."

"Well that was a no-brainer," he said as he let out his breath. "You were the only one nice to me. You let me sit with you during lunch. You laughed at my corny jokes. You still do." He kissed the tip of her nose. "And you never joined in with other people when they made fun of me."

She turned her gaze away. "The plan." She sighed. "I came up with that because I was afraid." She took a deep breath and kept on going. "I was afraid that if I told you how I truly felt that you would laugh at me."

For the life of him, Ned couldn't hold his laughter in any longer. He let out a full belly laugh that made Fiona's eyes go wide.

"See? This is what I mean." She jerked to her feet and headed to the door before Ned stopped her by grabbing her wrist.

"Wait. I'm not laughing at you, babe." He brought her down to the couch again. "I'm laughing at me. I went along with your plan thinking that this would be the only way a sexy woman like you would even consider going out with a guy like me." He laughed again. "We are too much alike to be good for anyone else."

This time she did laugh. "Ned, I'm sorry I didn't tell you how I really felt about being a lawyer. I thought if you knew I wanted to be a chef, you would have thought I was still that flaky cheerleader people used to laugh at in high school. I'm not a flake. Cooking is my passion."

"And you're damn good at it. You're right for going with your heart. Choose a career that will make you happy."

"But because I waited too long to tell you, you ruined your only chance at making it big at your job. It's my fault Chunti has your idea. I'm so sorry."

He smiled. "I should thank you. It's because of how I felt about you that made me tell Chunti my idea. If I hadn't done that, I wouldn't be going back to work to a job I want this time." He told her about the offer Hedrow made and she screamed in delight.

Wrapping her arms around his neck, she kissed the side of his face, his lips, his nose, any part of his face that she could get to. She was even happier to hear that the training would be in Maine.

"I've seen pictures. It's so beautiful there." She stroked his cheek.

"What about Kristoff?"

"I'll figure something out with him. He knows how I feel about you. He won't stand in my way. I know it."

"And tell me again how you feel." He just loved hearing her say it.

"I love you, Ned Cholurski. I love you with all of my heart and soul. I've known I've loved you since the minute I saw you walking into Mrs. Easton's French class, wearing that Metallica T-shirt and your faded black jeans. I had fallen more in love with you when you helped me with my homework. I had fallen in deeper when you allowed me to come live with you rent-free until I could find a job. And the first time we made love, I was gone. This last week has been miserable without you. If you need me to do another embarrassing cheer to get you back, I will. I'll do what it takes to get you back into my life."

"I only ask you for two things." He put his hand on her bare, smooth thigh. "Did you understand French better than me in high school?"

She bit her lower lip and hesitated to answer.

"Fi?"

She took a deep breath and spouted something that Ned thought translated to 'Claude has a cow in his yard.'

"What does that mean?" he asked.

"Ned is cute and has the most perfect lips I have ever seen." She smiled. "I said that all of the time to you and you didn't know what it meant."

"My mom did."

Her eyes went wide and she covered her mouth with her hand. "She must think I'm a slut or something."

"Or something. I told you. That woman loves you."

She held his hand. "What's the second thing?"

"Don't ever, ever lie to me again."

"I won't." She kissed him deeply, her tongue sliding into his mouth. Her hands combed through his thick hair as the other smoothed down his back.

When he pulled back from her, a smile on his face, he put his hand on her cheek, moved it down the side of her neck, down between her breasts and settled on her stomach.

"What Kwame said that day at the barbecue," he began. "Are you..."

She held his hand before he could ask the question. "C.C. said that she could tell I was pregnant. I told her that it was impossible. For one, I'm on the pill. Second, we had only had sex that week. No tests could show me pregnant that soon."

"But if you were?" he pressed.

She smiled. "I would love our baby with all of my heart."

He kissed her hard. "I love you so much, Fiona."

"Don't say it. Prove it."

Sliding his hands up her shirt, he almost touched her breasts when she stopped him. "Shouldn't we go back to the apartment? What if your parents come home?"

"They're playing bridge at Uncle Ivan's. They won't be home for hours. Besides, if we get caught that'll heighten the thrill." He pulled her onto his lap so that she faced him, her legs straddling him until his hard cock that strained against his shorts pressed against her wet sex. "So let's play naughty cheerleader and school-hero quarterback." He leaned in to kiss her and she stopped him with her fingers on his lips.

Shaking her head she said, "Oh, no. If we're role playing I want it to be the school cheerleader who's the valedictorian and the hunky brainiac who managed to come second in the class."

"You can call me a nerd. I don't mind. Not from you."

"Never. I love you too much to hurt you ever again."

He pulled her top over her head, a feat considering its tight fit. But what he found underneath stunned him. "Tell me you went braless when you wore this in high school."

She moved her mouth to his ear and whispered, "Only on the days I knew I would be studying with you."

He growled and turned her over onto her back on the couch.

"Not the old green-and-orange couch," she said as she pulled his T-shirt over his head.

"New furniture."

"Should we..."

"I'll buy them another fucking couch!"

His mouth covered hers as his hand massaged her breast. Behind his back, she kicked her shoes off, bouncing one on the coffee table and the other off of his back before it hit the floor.

"I can't believe you put this outfit on again." He kissed down her face to her neck. "Do you know how many fantasies I've had with you wearing this?"

"It wasn't easy to get back into, either. I've grown some tits and ass since then."

His mouth reached her breast and before he covered it, he said, "Thank God!"

He sucked on her luscious tit while massaging the other. Then he moved his mouth over to the other breast and massaged the one he just laved with his tongue. He moved down her stomach then found the side zipper on her skirt.

"Hurry up! Get me out of this thing. I can barely breathe."

He unzipped her and ripped the skirt and panty combo down her legs to her babydoll socks still covering her feet.

"Take the socks off," she said when his hand reached her feet.

He tossed the skirt to the side but shook his head. "Keep the socks on."

"Kinky!"

She pulled down his shorts but before he could position himself between her legs, she pushed him off of the couch and onto the floor so that he landed on his back. She straddled him and held his shaft.

"I still feel funny about fucking on your parents' new furniture."

"By all means, do what makes you feel comfortable."

Holding him, she stroked up, easing her hand up and down the long shaft, licking her lips as she noticed its beauty. Then she positioned herself over him, rubbing the thick tip against her lower lips until they both moaned out of ecstasy and agony.

"Baby."

It was all he needed to say before she plunged herself down on him. She held onto his shoulders as she gyrated her hips, moving him in and out of her.

His legs trembled when he felt he would pop soon but he held back. He wanted this time to last. He wanted to please Fiona. Holding onto her hips, he moved her up and down on his cock. She was so incredibly tight, drawing him in with every thrust and holding him there each time he drew out.

Looking at her, he didn't think it was possible to fall even more in love with her like the way Fiona had described falling for him in layers. But he had. With her silly little getup and her open and honest admission, he had fallen even harder for the beauty with brains.

"Oh God! Oh God! Neddy! Neddy!" She pounded her fists on his chest. Her body quivered and he knew her orgasm wasn't too far off. Thank God. He didn't know how long he could keep holding out.

"I love you, Fi!"

She screamed, leaned her head back and clamped her pussy walls around him so tight that he couldn't hold out for much longer and came in just as an explosive manner as her orgasm.

"Marry me, Ned!" she said in between pants. "Marry me."

"Yes. Damn, baby, yes."

She collapsed on top of him, breathless but definitely satisfied. "Thank you, sweetie."

"For what?"

He removed her wig, part of it still in its pigtails while the rest hung free and loose over her head, and stroked her real hair. Even with it plastered to her head, he loved the soft feel of it.

"For loving me even after all I've done. For going along with all of my crazy plans. For giving me the best sex I've ever had in my life."

"Hey, that's what friends are for."

**THE END**

**About the Author:**

Before you can say, "She can't go there with that story!" Bridget Midway is already taking you there and then some. Currently living in Virginia, Bridget writes erotica and erotic romances with multi-racial characters and usually with interracial romances. Differences should be celebrated, shared and explored, not seen as taboo. When she's not writing, she's writing and writing and, oh, writing some more. To read about her upcoming events, read her latest news, participate in her contest or read exclusive excerpts, go to her website at www.BridgetMidway.com. She also enjoys hearing from readers. Drop her a line at Bridget@BridgetMidway.com or read her blog at http://bridgetmidway.blogspot.com

# Liquid Silver Books
LSbooks.com

## Silver Net Community - meet our authors
LSbooks.net

## *The Best of LSB Romance...*

**The Zodiac Series**
*24 LSB Authors*
  12 books, a book a month from March 2005, each book
featuring two stories about that month's Zodiac star sign.
  http://zodiacromance.com

**Ain't Your Mama's Bedtime Stories**
*Best Anthology of 2003 - The Romance Studio*
  R. A. Punzel Lets Down Her hair - Dee S. Knight
  Beauty or the Bitch - Jasmine Haynes
  Snow White and the Seven Dorks - Dakota Cassidy
  Little Red, The Wolf, and The Hunter - Leigh Wyndfield
  Once Upon a Princess - Rae Morgan
  Petra and the Werewolf - Sydney Morgann
  Peter's Touch - Vanessa Hart

**Resolutions**
*4 ½ Stars Top Pick - Romantic Times BookClub*
    A Losing Proposition - Vanessa Hart
    Free Fall - Jasmine Haynes
    For Sale by Owner - Leigh Wyndfield
    That Scottish Spring - Dee S. Knight

## *More Contemporary Romances from LSB...*

**Love Lessons**
*Vanessa Hart*
    When solid friendship and passion collide, love is inevitable. This is the unexpected lesson for Wendy and Scott when she agrees to tutor him in the bedroom so he can try to win back his wayward wife.

**Impatient Passion**
*Dee S. Knight*
    A few day off turning thirty-five and life sucks. Austin needs to make big changes. When an anonymous stranger pulls her close on the bus, she chooses to indulge. Austin isn't anonymous to Tyler though. He's waited long enough, now it's time to claim the woman he's yearned for.

## Club Belle Tori
*Michelle Hoppe*

These two have it all, in spades. Jason Hunter has it all, in diamonds. Tori Lane has it all, in clubs. When their two best friends shuffle them together, can the millionaire and the pleasure palace owner have it all together, in hearts? Book I of the Club Belle Tori trilogy deals romance, passion, sexuality … and wild cards.

## Evening Star
*Rita Sable*

When Lilly takes a one-night job posing as an escort at a millionaire's party, she finds out that Gabe is more than she can handle...and everything she wants in a man.

## One Touch
*Susie Charles*

For Jake Reilly, one touch was all it took, and now he wants more, much more. Now Cassie's unrequited love for him is getting requited—real quick! When he discovers her secret, can he ever forgive her and will their growing feelings be strong enough to survive it?

## Single Station
*Rebecca Williams*

Rory McKenna is no farm boy. He's too pretty for one thing and his approach to seduction is out of this world. Rory takes Samantha places she never knew existed. How far can a farm girl go before it's too late to come back?

## Racing Hearts
*Rae Monet*

Cassandra's beauty is matched only by her raw driving talent and ambition. Stock car legend Justin is in financial straits. A perfect setup for a tycoon desperate to revive her cosmetics empire. Too desperate—can Justin keep Cassandra alive long enough for their passion to blossom?

## Undressing Mercy
*Deanna Lee*

Tricked into posing for Shamus, Mercy finds both her career and her body in his very capable hands. Soon Shamus realizes that his interest is far more personal than professional, and he's breaking his own rules and discovering that there is something very different about undressing Mercy

629745

Made in the USA